The Spanish Letters

Mollie Hunter

The Spanish Letters

Kelpies

Kelpies is an imprint of Floris Books

First published in 1964 by Evans Brothers Ltd, London
First published in Kelpies in 1984
Published in 2003 by Floris Books

The publisher acknowledges a Lottery grant
from the Scottish Arts Council towards the
publication of this series.

British Library CIP Data available

ISBN 0–86315–412-3

Printed in Europe

To Doctor E. J. Gow and the staff of Dunain House Hospital with deep gratitude for all their kindness to me.

Contents

1. *Enter a Stranger*

Late in the afternoon of a day near the end of January in the year 1589, an odd-looking trio of figures stood beside the Market Cross in Edinburgh's High Street. One was a bent old man leaning on a golf club — or cleek, as this was more commonly called in Scotland. A boy with tow-coloured hair and alert grey eyes stood at his side, and behind these two towered a massively-built man whose gentle features were in strange contradiction to the brutal strength of his physique. All three were shabby to the point of raggedness and their idle pose was belied by the sharp gaze of their eyes scanning the High Street.

Attentive as they all were to the busy comings and goings of the great thoroughfare, it was the boy, Jamie Morton, who first spied the tall young man on the brown horse riding towards them. Quickly he pointed him out to the other two.

"He is a stranger, that fellow on the brown horse," he commented. "See how he turns his head this way and that, seeking with his eyes."

The Cleek, as the old man was nick-named from the club that he constantly carried, peered after the boy's pointing finger. His leathery old face wrinkled in a grin of approval as he too noted how the rider carried himself.

"Aye, ye've sharp eyes, Jamie. Yon tall lad has never seen Edinburgh before."

Tod Carmichael, the big man, laughed. "Ye trained the laddie well, Cleek." He closed strong hands over Jamie's shoulders with another rumble of kindly laughter shaking his big frame. "You will earn your fee for the day yet, Jamie, if the stranger is needing a guide."

Jamie nodded, and in silence after that they watched the young man skilfully handling the brown horse up the street towards the Market Cross. An east wind blew keenly round them as they waited. Jamie shivered back from it and glanced enviously at the braziers glowing in the booths of the goldsmiths against the wall of Saint Giles's church on his right. For nearly a week past he had felt that same wind adding its misery of cold to his more accustomed ache of hunger. Now, as it probed icily through the thin stuff of his doublet, he had to summon all the courage of his fifteen years to face the prospect that the stranger might need no guide. There would be no fee then and so no food for him that night except the little that Tod and the Cleek would spare him in charity.

He turned to face the street again, grateful for Tod's protecting warmth at his back as he braced himself against the wind. The brown horse forged closer, then the stranger was up at the Market Cross and reining in to look down at them.

Seen thus close he proved to have strong, regular features, a light brown beard fashionably short and pointed and the sun-browned skin of one who has spent much time in the open air. The eyes of the three ragged figures at the Cross travelled swiftly from the handsome face to the fashionable velvet cloak and the well-cut leather of his riding-boots, and with long-accustomed skill they made their rapid assessment of the traveller.

"An elegant gallant," was Jamie's first thought. Then noting the watchful expression in the stranger's face and the military set of his broad shoulders under the fashionable cloak, he followed this up with a cautious, "— but no fool!"

"He has ridden hard," Tod whispered in his ear, and Jamie nodded agreement. The stranger's fine boots were thickly splattered with mud and the brown horse was lathered and shivering. The Cleek gave him a civil good-day to which the stranger replied before he said:

"I am seeking the lodging of John Forbes, Master of Fence. Can you direct me?"

He was English by his voice and his tones had a sharp sound of command that matched well with the soldierly way he carried himself. Neither Tod nor the Cleek responded to it, however, and stepping forward Jamie laid hold of the horse's bridle.

"'Tis not far," he said briskly. "I will guide you."

With a gesture of his whip the Englishman acknowledged his offer. He touched knees to his mount and as they moved off together up the High Street he asked: "What was that curious instrument the old man with you was carrying?"

"'Tis used in the game of golf," Jamie answered, and with a touch of condescension for the English ignorance of such a popular pastime, he explained the use of the cleek. "The old man played a very skilful game of golf in his youth," he added, "but now he uses the cleek only as a prop to his age and, when the need arises, as a weapon."

The Englishman's eyebrows went up at the last phrase, but he only said, "Neither he nor the big man seemed anxious to guide me."

"They have eaten today. My belly is still to fill," Jamie said frankly.

"You are very honest-spoken," the Englishman commented. He smiled with this remark and Jamie noticed that he was a very pleasant-looking young man with the hard watchfulness of his face thus softened. He smiled in reply.

"You will find none in Edinburgh to speak their minds as honestly as the caddies."

"The caddies?" the stranger queried. "Who are they?"

"Those like myself that ply for hire as messengers and porters," Jamie explained.

He pointed ahead to a narrow lane opening off the High Street on their right. "There is our way now. Down Beith's Wynd."

They swung into the alley he had indicated and halfway down it he turned the horse into an even narrower opening that led into a courtyard enclosed by houses towering eight and nine storeys high above them.

"This is Fisher's Close," he said, "and there straight ahead of you is Master Forbes's house."

The Englishman craned upwards at the tall house-fronts. "You build high in Edinburgh," he remarked.

"There is no room to build outwards an we are to keep safe within the city walls," Jamie told him seriously.

"Safe from whom?" The Englishman tossed the query out lightly, smiling again as he dismounted and handed the reins for Jamie to hold. For a second the boy hesitated in face of that friendly smile, but the habit of forthright speech was strong upon him.

"The English," he said bluntly.

The smile vanished from the Englishman's face. "You *do* speak your mind," he said, and then slowly, "That could be dangerous, boy."

Uneasily Jamie noted the stiffening of his face into the watchful mask he had first glimpsed at the Cross, but his had been a hard schooling in the life of the streets and he did not flinch from the forbidding stare of the blue eyes that met his own.

How the incident might have finished was left in doubt, however, for the tension between them was suddenly broken by the emergence of two figures into the courtyard. The first was a young girl, neatly but elegantly dressed in black with a small coif of white lace on her smooth dark hair, and striding close behind her an enormously tall man, red-haired and red-bearded with one hand resting on the hilt of the great sword that swung by his side.

It was the man particularly who drew the Englishman's attention, and involuntarily Jamie smiled at the astonished face he turned on the approaching pair. Angus Mhor, the Highlandman, with his flaming hair and beard and bare, brawny arms and legs projecting from the length of tartan cloth crudely kilted round his waist, was a familiar sight in Edinburgh, but clearly the Englishman had never seen his like before.

"And who, by the Great Harry, are these two," he demanded.

"Mistress Marie Forbes, daughter to the fencing-master, and the serving-man who guards her," Jamie told him. "He is a Highlandman — Angus Mhor they call him, 'mhor' being the Gaelic word for 'big.'"

"Gaelic? That is the Highland language, is it not?" the Englishman asked curiously.

"Aye," Jamie shrugged, "but Angus does not speak it now, nor any other. He is dumb from a blow on the head he got at the Battle of Liège when he was soldiering in the Netherlands with Master Forbes."

The oddly matched pair had disappeared inside the Forbes house by now and the Englishman turned from watching them. "Why should he guard the girl?" he asked. "Is her life in danger?"

"Sometimes," Jamie said. "Her mother was a Frenchwoman who had a great skill in herbs. She used to doctor the poor of the city and now that she is dead Mistress Marie does the same. It is work that takes her into rough places and her father will only allow it if Angus Mhor goes with her."

"She will be safe enough with that massive fellow by her side," the Englishman commented.

"Aye," Jamie agreed. "The fencing master saved his life in the fighting at Liège and now the Highlandman lives only to serve him and Mistress Marie."

The Englishman turned a speculative look on him. "You know a great deal!"

"There is not much I do not know about Edinburgh."

It was not a boast on Jamie's part but a simple statement of fact. The Englishman continued to look shrewdly at him as if weighing the words in relation to some thought of his own but, "Wait here," was all he said at last. Turning on his heel he went up to the door of Forbes's house. It opened under his knocking, the fat figure of Nan, the Forbes's serving-girl appeared for a moment and he followed her in.

As Jamie watched him disappear the sharp pains of hunger twisted his stomach again suddenly and for a moment his head swam. He leant against the lathered flank of the horse and the feeling subsided. It was quiet in the courtyard and sheltered from the cold wind and with his head against the horse's warm flank Jamie felt a peaceful languor steal over him. He must have dozed then, for he had no recollection of time passing till he heard Nan's shrill voice calling to him from the doorway. Still half-dazed he looped the reins over a tethering post and stumbled towards her.

"The master wants you, Jamie," she told him. "He is in there — in the *salle d'armes*."

The French phrase tumbled clumsily out in her broad Scots voice but Jamie heard it with a sharp thrill of excitement. The *salle d'armes* of Master John Forbes was a place he had long dreamed of but never hoped to enter, and with quickened heartbeat he pushed open the door she indicated.

Neither of the two men in the room beyond saw him enter, so hotly engrossed were they in argument. The fencing master, iron-grey hair awry with the fierce thrusting of his hands through it, beard jutting defiantly as he looked up to the Englishman's taller height, was talking in low urgent tones. He paced a step or two back and forward; and as he had done many times before in the streets, Jamie watched admiringly the light movements that proclaimed the master swordsman.

The secret memory of his own long hours of practice with any weapon he could beg or borrow sent his eyes roving over the racks of foils and *épées*, the gleaming silver of sabres that lined the walls, and envy overwhelmed him. What would he not give, he thought yearningly, for one lesson from Master Forbes — one lesson with the deadly beauty of one of these blades gleaming in his hand and the voice of the greatest fencing master in Europe to instruct him!

The Englishman's voice raised in angry protest brought his attention back to the other two. "I *cannot* do as you advise," he was saying loudly. "It would be in direct contrary to my instructions to admit any but yourself to my confidence."

Forbes swung on his heel as if to walk away in disgust and saw Jamie standing in the doorway.

"Ah, here *is* Jamie!" he exclaimed. "Come here, boy."

Cautiously Jamie advanced over the long stretch of polished wooden floor. Forbes took him by the shoulders and turned him round to face the Englishman.

"This is Mr Roger Macey, Jamie," he said. "He is here in Edinburgh on business and I wish to persuade him that the caddies are like to be of great service to him."

"Why yes, sir!" Jamie responded eagerly. "I will fetch and carry for you, find you a lodging, hire you a horse, nurse you when you are sick —"

"I have told him all this," Forbes broke in impatiently. "He knows by now the way the caddies gain their bread. But his business is secret, Jamie. Do you understand?"

The meaning of the conversation dawned on Jamie. He looked up at the Englishman again and unconsciously straightening his shoulders as he spoke said: "We caddies happen on many strange things as we go hither and thither in the city, but we are sworn never to reveal the business of any who may employ us. Even among ourselves we may only tell as much as is necessary to further that business."

"You see, Macey!" Forbes broke in again. "They have their own rules of conduct. That old man you saw — the Cleek — he is the leader of their brotherhood —"

"— and we are sworn also to stand by one another, not only in sickness but in any danger that may arise from the pursuit of our calling," Jamie took up the tale. "So you see, Mr Macey, poor as we are it is well known there is no one in Edinburgh more worthy of trust than the caddies."

"And take advantage of it, all of you, with your outspoken manner!" Forbes added. He turned again to Macey. "I tell you Macey, your business would be safer with the caddies than your purse would be in the vault of a goldsmith! And where would you find their equal for knowledge of the city? Take my advice, man, for pity's sake, or I warn you, you will finish up as poor Norton may have done."

Abruptly Macey turned from them and paced up and down. He was plainly more than half-convinced but he made one last stand.

"The boy is too young for my purpose," he protested.

"Oh give me patience!" Forbes exploded. "Do you not see, man, Jamie is young enough to pass unnoticed where the presence of a grown man would excite suspicion? Yet he is a strong lad, well-grown for his years and quick-witted. His age is perfectly matched to your purpose."

Macey threw up his hands in capitulation. "Very well, Forbes. As matters have turned out thus with Norton I will risk the censure of my principals and take your advice."

"You will not regret it, Mr Macey," Jamie said eagerly. "I will find a lodging for you now and —"

"No, Jamie," Forbes interrupted. "Mr Macey will lodge here — I insist." He held up a hand to silence Macey's polite protest. "My daughter, Marie, is an excellent cook. She learned many French dishes from her poor mother (God rest her soul) that I am too Scottish to relish, and it will give her great delight to practise her fancy receipts on you."

"The delight will be mine, I assure you," Macey said gallantly.

"Then it is settled," Forbes decided. "My servant will stable your horse."

He went out calling, "Angus! Hither to me, Angus Mhor!" and left Jamie and Macey regarding one another in silence.

"I am looking for a man," Macey said at last, "a fellow called Ralph Norton, a ballad-singer who has been in Edinburgh this past two months."

"I know him well — we all do," Jamie said, "but I have not seen him for a few days now, or heard of him either."

"Nor has anyone, according to Master Forbes," Macey told him, "yet I know for certain that he has not left the city and so I fear he may have been the victim of foul play. However, alive or dead, I must find him. But be discreet in your questions. There must be no talk in the city that he is being sought."

"I understand," Jamie nodded. He turned to go but Macey's hand fell heavily on his shoulder. "Wait!" he said, and loosing the pouch at his belt he fished out a coin and pushed it into Jamie's hand.

"You will not search far on an empty belly, boy. Take this as earnest of your fee."

Jamie gaped at the coin gleaming silver in his palm. "There will be more than this to earn?" he asked incredulously.

"That will depend on what has happened to Norton," Macey replied.

He turned away again and for a moment Jamie hesitated, a question trembling on the tip of his tongue. As if he sensed this, Macey said over his shoulder, "Ask no questions, but go quickly, boy!"

It was the military voice again, the quick incisive tone of the officer giving a command, and instinctively Jamie reacted to it. Swiftly he left the house and raced back down Beith's Wynd and into the High Street again. The thought of the Cleek was uppermost in his mind. If anyone knew where to find the vanished Norton it would be that sly old man with his questing eyes and ancient head crammed full of the gossip of the city.

And yet Macey's advice had been shrewd, he thought, feeling the edge of the coin bite against his hand. It showed he had a good fund of common sense for all his fine clothes and gentleman's bearing! And stopping at the first bake-house he came to he exchanged part of his silver coin for a meat pie. It was not a very good pie, made with salt beef and probably the last of the barrel at that, Jamie thought, but still as his teeth broke the crust and the savoury juices trickled down his chin, the relief from hunger was exquisite.

Leaning against the bake-house wall as he ate he conned over the events of the past hour. Macey's "business" was a mysterious affair. What interest, after all, could an elegant young gallant with a military air have in a wandering ballad-singer like Ralph Norton? And why should Forbes take it on himself to advise Macey how to go about finding him? Why, indeed, had Macey gone to Forbes in the first place?

Well, Jamie thought, as he licked the last crumbs of the pie from his fingers, if he could not find these things out with the help of the brotherhood in addition to finding Norton, he would not be worthy of the title of caddie! And turning south he plunged into the warren of narrow streets that would bring him out into the street of Potterrow where the Cleek had his winter lodging.

2. Search for a Ballad-singer

The Cleek's cellar was warmed by the potter's kiln that burned day and night in a neighbouring cellar and there was just enough space in it for the four who shared it — the Cleek himself, Tod, Jamie, and one-legged Lucky Finlayson. The three others were there when Jamie entered that night but only Lucky was stretched out on the straw palliasses they unrolled nightly for sleep.

Tod was kneading gently at the muscles in the stump of Lucky's right leg and when Jamie came in he looked up to say quietly, "His leg is troubling him again."

The one-legged man stifled a groan. "Lucky to have one left," he said philosophically.

"Aye, Lucky, aye," Tod soothed him and went on with his gentle massage.

Jamie watched sympathetically, remembering Angus Mhor and his dumbness, for Lucky was also a veteran of the fighting in the Netherlands. The same battle in which Angus had lost his power of speech had cost Lucky his leg, but "lucky to have one left" was his invariable attitude to the fate of being a cripple and "Lucky" his byname in consequence. It was an attitude that showed the courage of the man, the Cleek always maintained, and knowing the pain that Lucky had to endure from the stump Jamie agreed with him.

He took his place beside the Cleek and waited till Tod was ready also to listen to him, then rapidly he recounted the conversation between Macey and Forbes and told of the task the Englishman had set him.

"You were the last to see Norton," the Cleek said to

Tod when he had finished speaking. "You had better tell the boy of it."

"It was a week ago," Tod said, "on the — let me see, aye it would be the four and twentieth day of this month. There was a gathering of some of the nobility late that night at the old de Guise palace —"

"— the de Guise palace?" Jamie asked, puzzled.

"Aye, the house that Lord John de Hope has now," Tod explained, "the one that stands at the end of Blair's Close, off the High Street."

"Ach, Lord de Hope only has the tenancy of it," the Cleek said impatiently. "It has been in the de Guise family ever since it was built long ago for the king's grandmother, Marie de Guise. Give the place its proper name!"

"The boy's young to know these things," Tod soothed the old man, and he subsided, grumbling to himself. "Anyway, Jamie," he went on, "Norton was engaged to play the lute and sing at a dinner these lords had there that night. I know this because I earned my supper that same night by waiting with a link to light them as they went up Blair's Close to the palace, and Norton told me as he went in that he was engaged to entertain them."

"But was that the last you saw of him?" Jamie asked.

"Aye," Tod nodded. "The lords that went in came out later on and one or two paid me for the light from my link as they passed. But Norton did not come out. And I will tell you another thing, Jamie. Lord de Hope came out with his guests. He left for France that night and the house has been shut up ever since — not even a servant was left there."

The three of them sat looking at one another in a silence that was broken at last by the Cleek saying flatly, "If Norton did not come out of the palace it was because he could not. Norton is dead."

"Dead!" Jamie echoed. "But why should any of these noble lords kill a poor ballad-singer?"

"Listen, boy!" The Cleek thrust his seamed face close to Jamie's own. "Tod has told me who these lords were. The Earls of Huntly, Errol, and Crawford, and Lord Claude Hamilton — every one of them of the Roman faith. As Lord de Hope is himself. And this, boy, remember, is a Protestant country where the practice of the Roman faith has been outlawed since the Reformation. And now I will tell you something that I noticed for myself. Master Ralph Norton had too fine a manner of speech to be the poor ballad-singer that he pretended to be. Now, what d'ye make of that?"

Jamie looked from the Cleek's wrinkled face to Tod's big placid one, both pressed close to his in the light of the tallow dip on the wall.

"I — I am not practised in these things," he said helplessly. "You will have to tell me."

"Do not be-devil the boy, Cleek," Tod said gently. "What he means, Jamie, is that a meeting of Catholic lords late at night could mean that there was plotting of some kind afoot, and a man like Norton who was not all that he seemed to be was most likely a spy of some kind. Put the two together and you will see that if they found him out then he will have paid the price of his kind."

"But they cannot have left him lying dead inside the house!" Jamie exclaimed. "Lord de Hope must wish to return there, sometime — surely they would have had to carry his body away with them!"

"There is the Nor Loch," Tod pointed out. "The garden at the back of the palace reaches right down to the water's edge."

Jamie gasped. "Hah!" the Cleek exclaimed. "You see now, eh?"

It was all too plain, Jamie thought. That stretch of shallow, reedy water bounding Edinburgh on its northern edge was a deserted place in the winter months. A body could float there for long enough before it was noticed and be unrecognisable before it was found.

The touch of the Cleek's bony hand on his arm startled him out of his reverie. "Jamie," the old man said seriously, "Norton was an Englishman, as you know, and he may well have been a spy for some reason or some person that we do not know. Now here comes another Englishman enquiring secretly after his fate. Take care, Jamie. There may be trouble in the wind, for it runs in my head that this Macey is a spy also!"

"An English spy," Tod added, "and England has always been the enemy of our country. Take very great care, Jamie!"

With a sense of shock Jamie realized that his two oldest and best friends were looking at him almost with an air of menace. "D'you think I would forget any sooner than you that I am Scottish born and bred?" he said hotly.

The Cleek's eyes flashed a warning of anger at his tone but Tod, whose anger was as rare as it was formidable, silenced him with a gesture. "You are young, and your experience of these things is not great, that is all," he said mildly.

Jamie, however, was still resentful. "I will tell him what has happened to Norton for I have taken his fee to do so," he snapped, "but if you think I would aid an English spy you are sadly mistaken!"

He rolled over on to his palliasse and stretched out. The voices of Tod and the Cleek muttered on mingling with the uneasy breathing of Lucky restlessly asleep in his corner, and deliberately Jamie tried to shut them out of his hearing. Gradually the sounds faded from his ears and sleep overtook him.

He awoke again in darkness but although there was no light in the cellar instinct told him that day had begun. The other three still slept, and carefully picking his way past them he climbed the cellar steps into the street again.

It was barely light yet but this suited his purpose. The less light there was on the search for Norton's body the better it would be for all concerned, he thought grimly, and the hot little flame of anger kindled in his mind last night against Macey, the English spy, flared up again.

Swiftly he made his way again to Forbes's house, and in the courtyard outside waited patiently for the servant, Nan, to make her morning trip for water from the public well. She came out shortly after he arrived, and yawning and shivering she yoked the water-buckets round her neck, only to drop them again with a clatter as Jamie glided silently up to her.

"Hold your noise, Nan," he said impatiently, "and go and tell the Englishman I am here. Quickly, you understand, and quietly. And he must come quickly too."

She gaped at him, then her stupid, good-natured face broke into a friendly grin. "Eh, ye're a wee devil, Jamie," she exclaimed. "Some mischief ye're up to, I'll be bound." But she kilted up her skirts willingly enough, all the same, and ran back to the house.

Minutes later Macey appeared, cloak over his arm and fastening up the laces of his doublet as he came. "Norton?" he demanded crisply, striding towards Jamie.

The boy nodded. "Follow me," he said. "I will take you by back ways and we can talk as we go."

Macey fell into step behind him. "What has happened? Is he alive?" he demanded.

"I do not think so," Jamie said over his shoulder, and rapidly as they walked he gave Macey the bare facts of what Tod had told him. Macey made no comment and he asked no questions, and Jamie himself said nothing of the speculation that had passed between him and the other caddies.

There was little opportunity to talk in any case. Their way led in a downward-sloping direction away from the High Street and through one narrow alley after another, often with barely room to pass between the houses, always picking their way round the piled heaps of refuse outside them, and sometimes with the additional hazard to avoid of pigs that rooted in the garbage.

They came out on to the shores of the Nor Loch at last, however, and as they stood to recover their breath Jamie briefly explained the geography of their position to the Englishman.

"We are facing north now," he said, pointing to the water stretching east and west in front of them, "and this is the city's northern boundary — the Nor Loch." A sweeping gesture of his hand took in the huddled ranks of tall houses ascending the slope behind them. "The loch and the High Street lie parallel to one another, both running east and west," he went on, "and these houses lie in between the two."

"I have studied Hertford's map of the city," Macey said, "but you put it clearly. Now lead on, boy, wherever we are going."

"That I cannot tell exactly," Jamie said frankly, "except that we must take a line on that tall building there."

"The de Guise palace you spoke of?" Macey looked

up and to the left at the ornate towers and cupolas of the palace standing clear of the citizen's houses crowding down the slope towards the water.

"Unless they have buried him in the palace gardens!" Jamie said, struck suddenly by the possibility.

Macey laughed shortly. "A group of earls stoop to soil their hands with the spadework of burying a ballad-singer? There were no servants left in the house, remember. No, your friends were right. If poor Ralph is dead it is in the waters of the loch we will find him."

He moved off, squelching along the marshy verge, thrusting the reeds and bushes aside as he went, and Jamie followed, wincing as the cold water of the marsh seeped through the broken leather of his shoes. When they were in line with the de Guise palace, Macey stopped. The gardens sloping upwards to the palace started some thirty feet back from the water's edge and were raised at this point some four feet above the level of the bank of the loch. Low scrub grew in the space between the water and the vertical wall of smooth turf that marked the beginning of the gardens.

Macey leant against this wall for a few moments. In the early morning light he looked so haggard that Jamie felt a sudden compassion for him. "*Poor Ralph,*" he had called Norton, and remembering this it occurred to Jamie that the man must have been his friend.

"If you wait here," he offered, "I will search for him."

"No!" Macey jerked the word out vehemently as he thrust himself away from the wall. In a quieter tone he added: "You are too young, in any case, to look upon death — if he *is* dead."

With a shrug Jamie said, "You need not fear for that.

I have looked on death many times since my parents died."

"You are an orphan then," Macey commented.

"My parents died together of the plague some seven years ago," Jamie told him. "The Cleek found me wandering in the streets and taught me how to gain my bread."

"H'm. You are a bright lad. 'Tis pity you have no chance to learn a trade," Macey went on absent-mindedly.

"'Tis no pity at all!" Jamie gave a little snort of laughter with the words. "I do not wish to be bound to a trade! True, I earn little as a caddie and often I am cold and hungry. But I am free, Mr Macey, and I call no man my master."

"Then you wish to be a caddie all your life?" Macey asked, and suddenly Jamie realized that neither this question nor any possible answer to it was of any interest to his companion. His eyes were directed to the water's edge, and following their line Jamie saw a flutter of cloth among the reeds. The Englishman was simply talking to delay the moment when he would have to go forward and investigate what lay there.

Macey caught the look the boy gave him. Bleak-faced, he moved forward and bent down to part the reeds. The body behind them was almost completely submerged in the water. Macey bent and heaved at it and it came up with a suck and a splash from the mud that held it. It lay face upwards. Quickly Macey dropped his cloak over the sightless face. With hands that shook he unfastened the front of his doublet and pulled the garment open, and bending over his shoulder Jamie saw that Norton had died of stab wounds in the chest.

"He died facing them — and only a lute in his hand! Oh, Ralph! My poor Ralph!"

At the muffled anguish in Macey's voice Jamie turned and retreated a few steps. Whoever and whatever Macey was, he realized, this was a grief that should not be intruded on. He could not avoid a look, however, and somewhat to his surprise saw Macey lift his head again and with quick, purposeful fingers begin a systematic search of the dead man's clothing.

Presently he straightened himself and stood up. He walked over to Jamie. "I do not wish this man's death to be known," he said harshly, "nor do I wish my presence in the city to be linked in any way with him. Therefore I cannot remove his body from this place by myself. Yet I cannot leave him thus, for he was my friend. Is there any way he can be taken hence by stealth and secretly given decent Christian burial?"

"The caddies can arrange it," Jamie said quietly. "There is a man of God in the city whom they saved once from his enemies at a time of religious strife. He will bury your friend for them, secretly, but with due Christian reverence."

In tones that shook slightly Macey said, "I will pay well for the charity of such a deed."

He bent his head and stood as if lost in thought. When he looked up again the emotion he had shown earlier was gone and his face was once more controlled and purposeful.

"I have another task for you, boy," he began. "There is a man called Sempill — a Colonel William Sempill whom I —"

"No!" Jamie interrupted him. "I will have no more of your tasks!"

"What is this?" Macey's face flamed with the suddenness of his anger. "You are poor and I have offered to pay you well!"

"I am not so poor as to offer my honour for sale!" Jamie retorted.

"Your honour! What nonsense is this?" Macey shouted angrily.

But composedly ignoring the angry face bent down on him Jamie turned away with the words, "My honour as a Scotsman and a loyal subject of King James. I will not serve an English spy!"

3. *A Bargain*

He had taken only two steps when Macey had pinioned him from behind in a grip that locked agonisingly round the muscles of his upper arms.

As Tod had taught him to do in such a case, Jamie swung backwards with his right foot using his left foot as a pivot and his right shoulder as the lever to swing his opponent's weight round. The Englishman knew the move. He came up and over, landing lightly on his feet, and they faced one another, crouched, hands advanced for the next grip.

"I was taught my wrestling by a Cumberland man," Macey said between his teeth, "and I have ten years more practice at the art than you have!"

It was the situation in a nutshell, and yielding to the inevitable, Jamie dropped his hands. "You cannot force me to work for you all the same," he retorted. He straightened up, and dropping his guard also, Macey followed suit.

"We could come to terms," he suggested, and as Jamie opened his mouth to protest, "No, wait! I will not ask you to do anything to offend your conscience."

"That cannot be," Jamie objected. "Your country is enemy to mine and always has been."

"Answer me one question," Macey said. "Do you think Master Forbes would be traitor in any way to Scotland?"

"Never!" Jamie exclaimed, and stopped short as the implication struck home. The fencing master was Macey's ally — yet it was unthinkable that *he* should work against king and country!

"I will put my cards on the table," Macey said. "I can

see that I must have the help of the caddies now that Norton is dead, and so I have no choice. Will you at least listen to me?"

He waited expectantly for a reply and Jamie considered him thoughtfully. Macey's build and skill, he was realising, would make it impossible for him to escape, and the longer he lingered there the more likely he was to be connected with the mystery of Norton's body among the reeds. On the other hand, he would lose nothing by listening to what Macey had to say, and in spite of Tod's and the Cleek's warning he was curious to learn more about him. Moreover, the anger he had felt the night before was gone now, dispelled by sympathy for Macey's genuine grief over Norton's death.

Cautiously he considered all these things, but in the end it was the honesty and obvious sincerity of Macey's appeal that moved him to a decision. Glancing towards the smoke rising from the chimney tops and other signs of life in the awakening city, he gestured in Norton's direction.

"It is better we do not linger here," he said. "We can talk in Master Forbes's house."

With a nod that tacitly accepted the 'we' of his comment, Macey left him to stride forward and arrange the reeds to hide Norton's body again. He straightened up, the cloak that had covered the dead man's face slung over his arm again.

"I cannot leave it here to connect me with him," he said, following Jamie's glance at it, and nodding agreement the boy said:

"It would look strange in any case for you to be abroad without a cloak on such a cold morning."

Neither of them spoke after that on the journey back to Forbes's house. Macey's brow was furrowed as if in deep thought, and glancing at him from time to time,

Jamie felt his curiosity growing. Whatever the reason for Norton's death, he reflected, it must have changed matters greatly for Macey to have him so grateful now for the help he had rejected so violently at first!

They were met just inside the doorway of Forbes's house by Marie Forbes. Nan was hovering behind her, still in her morning disarray of curling-rags and dirty apron, but Mistress Marie was as elegant and neatly-coiffed as always. And so self-possessed, thought Jamie with an inward smile, that it was hard to believe she was only eighteen months older than himself:

"Why, M'sieu Macey!" she exclaimed at their entrance. "You went out without breaking your fast! That is not good for you."

She looked accusingly past him to Jamie. "You are to blame," she said. "Nan has told me you came and said he must go quickly with you. That is not the way to treat our guest, Jamie!"

"'Tis no matter, Mistress Marie," Macey said smilingly, "and you are not to put yourself in a stir for me. I am not used to such care."

Marie, however, was not listening to him. She was still looking past him to Jamie, a flush of pink spreading over the ivory-paleness of her delicate features. "Why are you smiling, Jamie?" she demanded. "I did not speak to amuse you!"

"I am sorry, mistress," Jamie apologized. "It is just the way you say my name — *Zhaimee*."

"Oh!" she clasped her hands to her mouth with a flustered little gesture. "You make game of my French voice — it is not fair!"

"No, no, Mistress Marie, I like it fine!" Jamie protested, and Macey exclaimed in the same breath, "'Tis the prettiest manner of speech ever I heard!"

"And so say I!" Forbes's deep voice broke into their

united protest, bringing them all round to look at him standing in a doorway opening off the passage. "You are a goose, Marie," he said, dropping his arm affectionately round her shoulders, "but you have the prettiest voice in the land and I will spit any man through the heart that disputes it!"

"'Tis a stroke then that will never be dealt," Macey said gallantly. Forbes roared with laughter, and with the blush deepening in her face Marie pulled herself away from him.

"Come, Nan," she said, "you will take a tray of breakfast to the study for your master and M'sieu Macey."

With dignity, she retreated down the passage. They looked after her, Jamie and Macey still smiling and Forbes with a sudden serious expression on his face.

"She is her mother over again," he said, "pretty, proud, and the kindest heart in three kingdoms."

"You are fortunate, sir," Macey said politely. Forbes, nodding a grave assent, beckoned them to follow him into the study. With his back thus to them he was unaware that Macey's expression had changed as he looked after Marie's retreating form. But Jamie noticed the Englishman's face, and inwardly smiling again he thought to himself, "Why, he is smitten already with her charm!"

"What news?" Forbes asked.

"Norton is dead," Macey said soberly, and briefly he recounted the circumstances of his discovery.

Forbes heard him out, barely concealing his impatience, and at the end of the recital he said vehemently, "Then you *must* have the help of the caddies if you are to track down Sempill and d'Aquirre!"

"I know. I accept now that you were right," Macey agreed wearily, "and that is why the boy has returned here with me. But I have yet to convince him that it will not go against conscience to assist me, and so I have decided to put my cards on the table."

He paused as if to put his thoughts in order, then speaking directly to Jamie he went on: "Ralph Norton was my good friend. He was also — as I am — an agent of the English government, and he had sent information south to our superiors in London that two agents of King Philip of Spain had landed in Scotland and were reported to be active in Edinburgh. One of these is the Colonel William Sempill of whom I spoke, and the other is the man in black."

The last words had an ominous ring that caused Jamie to shiver suddenly. "Has he no other name, this man in black?" he queried.

"He goes by various names according to the circumstance of the moment," Macey said grimly, "and currently he is said to be using the name of M'sieur François d'Aquirre. But throughout the whole of Europe he is known as 'the man in black,' for he is always dressed from head to toe in that colour. And his heart is as black as his clothes — as the many people who have cause to fear and hate him will testify."

"And Colonel Sempill?" Jamie asked. "Who is he?"

"A Scot — a renegade Scot in the pay of Spain!" Forbes interjected violently.

The words were accompanied by a gesture of contempt that was frightening in its fierceness. Jamie looked enquiringly at Macey, but ignoring Forbes's interruption he went on:

"Norton also indicated to our superiors that he was on the verge of an important discovery about the activities of these two men. He asked that I be sent north to assist him and said that he could be reached through Master Forbes who, for reasons of his own, was also interested in tracking down Sempill."

He looked at the fencing master again at this point as if inviting him to speak, but Forbes remained silent and Jamie said:

"What you have told me is clear enough, but you have not yet made plain the reasons behind the spying on the activities of these two Spanish agents."

"Cast your mind back to the summer of last year," Macey invited, "when Philip of Spain's Great Armada attempted to land on England's shores. Do you remember the great fear in Scotland at that time that he would succeed in doing this and then invade your country also?"

"Aye, the warning beacons were standing all ready to be lit if it should happen that the English fleet was defeated," Jamie recalled, "and all the bells were rung for joy when news came that the Spanish ships had been driven off."

"The defeat has never ceased to rankle with the Spanish king," Macey said, "and the constant fear in England is that he will attempt another landing, for we have intelligence of great activity of ship-building in certain Spanish ports over the past months."

He looked searchingly at Jamie as he said this and then continued, "I tell you, boy, with things in such a case there would not be Spanish agents at work in Scotland now without good cause. And if that cause is to prepare the way for an attack by another Armada, then the caddies *must* help me to forestall their plans, for Philip is determined to conquer England in order to force it over to the Roman faith, and if he succeeds in this he will not long endure the existence of another Protestant country on his doorstep. The fall of England to the Spaniard will only be the prelude to the fall of your country also."

In the silence that followed this declaration they

heard the clatter of Nan's wooden pattens in the passage outside mingling with the lighter click of Marie's high leather heels. The door swung open and the servant came in ahead of her bearing a long tray of dishes that steamed aromatically.

"Set it down here, Nan," Marie ordered. Unceremoniously she cleared a confusion of papers from her father's work-table.

"There is food to break your fast in the kitchen, Jamie," she added as Nan set the tray down.

The meat pie of the night before was only a pleasant memory and with alacrity Jamie was making for the door when Forbes caught his arm. "Jamie is needed here, daughter," he said. "Nan can bring another bowl and spoon for him."

"To sup with yourself and M'sieu Macey?" Marie asked incredulously, but Forbes turned from her without reply and addressed himself to Jamie. "Give us your answer, Jamie," he said curtly. "Will you work with Mr Macey, giving him all the help that lies within the caddies' power?"

Jamie looked from one to the other of the faces regarding him — the girl and the serving-woman, bewildered by this reversal of the accepted domestic order, Macey and Forbes both grim and intent on the business in hand. It was on Macey that his eyes finally came to rest. The Englishman was standing lightly poised with one hand on his sword-hilt, his whole bearing expressive of the resolute man of action. He smiled as Jamie's eyes met his, the same frank, friendly smile that had preceded their battle of wills in the courtyard the day before.

"You may find yourself in danger," he said, "but you look like a lad that would relish the spice of danger and the work will be well paid. Is the bargain struck?"

The last vestige of doubt vanished from Jamie's mind with the words. Macey's argument had been clear and sound, he decided, and the lure of adventure he held out now was something that could not be resisted. Impulsively he held out his hand.

"The bargain is struck," he said cheerfully.

"And held!" Macey responded, taking the proffered hand in a firm clasp, and gripping their clasped hands with his own Forbes finished, "And sealed!"

At the sight of her father, the strange Englishman and the grimy street-boy all clasping hands, a bewildered exclamation escaped from Marie. It was an oddly feminine sound to follow so closely on such a traditionally masculine ceremony, and the effect was comic enough to impel Jamie and the men into a burst of laughter. Still laughing, Forbes detached himself from the group and came across to her.

"Be off for the bowl!" he ordered Nan. She scurried off and smiling down at Marie he said, "We are not mad, as you think, my love, and presently I will explain to you what we are engaged in. But for the meantime, Jamie will be staying here. Nan can bring a truckle bed into the kitchen for him, and he is to have access to myself and Mr Macey at any time he desires. You understand?"

"But perfectly," Marie answered. She had regained her composure by this time and looking Jamie up and down with a critical eye she added, "If this boy is to be a member of my household he must go warmly and decently clad. I will see what I can find to take the place of that doublet — it is outgrown and too thin for this bitter weather."

"That is my good daughter," Forbes said affectionately, and watching once again how his eyes followed her as she left him Jamie thought to himself, "I would not care to be in the shoes of anyone who harmed that man's daughter!"

Macey brought them all back to the business in hand with a brisk, "And now to business, Forbes! Norton did not say what your interest is in Sempill and you have not declared it to me. Will you do so now?"

"No," Forbes answered flatly, "I will not! You wish to find Sempill and so do I. Therefore I will do everything in my power to help you, but my business with him concerns nobody but myself."

It seemed to Jamie that all the goodwill in the room was suddenly shattered with the words. Forbes stood with bearded chin out-thrust, defiance written on his face, and though Macey was in control of his emotions his expression was forbidding.

"Be careful our purposes do not cross, Forbes," he said dangerously. "I have come far and risked much to find this man and I *will* find him."

"I had better know how he looks," Jamie broke in uneasily. "Can you tell me fairly how he is built and coloured?"

"Macey has never seen him," Forbes answered, "but I know him well and I can tell you that he is a year or two younger than myself. He is well above the middle height and strong built. He has a straight carriage and his hair and beard are a golden-red colour. And he is a good swordsman — almost as good as myself."

The thought that had been stirring in Jamie's brain for the last few minutes took sudden fire from Forbes's final words. It was difficult for him to find words to express it, however, and awkwardly aware of the flush creeping over his face he said, haltingly,

"Master Forbes, I am eager to learn the art of swordsmanship. Lucky Finlayson has taught me something of it already and I have practised much, but if you would condescend to one lesson —"

His voice trailed off under Forbes's look, but the strength of his longing overcame the feeling of awkwardness and he added, "Mr Macey has promised me a good fee and I would gladly pay all of it for one lesson from you."

"So the sparrow of the streets would become a fighting-cock!" Forbes commented, and to Jamie's embarrassment he gave a sudden great burst of laughter in which Macey joined.

Utterly humiliated at the sound, he made for the door, only to find his way blocked by Nan returning with the extra bowl and spoon. Forbes's hand reached out over his shoulder and took them from her, and with the other hand he drew Jamie back.

"The idea is not too far-fetched, Forbes," Macey said. "He is a strong lad and with a little skill in his sword-arm could be useful in a brawl. I will pay for the lessons over and above his fee."

The words had a condescending ring in Jamie's ears and sudden furious resentment against the two fine gentlemen who had laughed at his cherished dream overwhelmed his shame in a burst of rage. Wrenching himself free of Forbes's clasp he said defiantly to Macey:

"I will take what I earn from you and not a penny more!" And whirling round on Forbes he hurled at him: "And as for you, I will push that laughter back down your throat one day — with the point of a sword! Master-swordsman as you are, I swear I will better your own weapon yet!"

There was a silence in which Forbes set the bowl and spoon down on the table with elaborate care. Watching him, Jamie thought dismally of the beating one of those strong arms could administer, but the anger of the moment was still hot on him and he was determined not to retract his defiance.

"Your pardon, Jamie. I did not mean to offend," Macey said quietly, and as Forbes turned to them, "There is good stuff in the boy, Forbes. The fee I have in mind will cover the lessons if you will consent to give them."

Forbes looked at them both with expressionless face. "You are a hot-tempered, unruly boy, Jamie Morton," he said at last, "and the only reason I have not beaten you senseless already is that I cannot make up my mind whether to take a whip or a stick to you."

He paused for a moment to let this have the desired impact before he said, "But even so, you have the courage to speak thus to John Forbes!"

With a sudden characteristic gesture he thrust his powerful bearded face forward. "But I will make no bargain with you," he finished, "till you have found Sempill. Then we can talk of swordsmanship!"

4. The Men of Liège

"I think," Macey suggested, "that we all understand one another well enough now — and here is Mistress Marie's excellent cooking lying quite neglected!" And with a deft movement that intruded himself between Forbes and Jamie he took the fencing master's arm and drew him towards the breakfast table.

As he had meant them to, the words and the action that went with them reduced the atmosphere to a more normal tone, and the surface politeness required in supping together helped to further the diplomatic intention. Breakfast, accordingly, finished on a note of calm discussion for which Jamie at least was thankful, his previous formal acquaintance with Master Forbes not having prepared him to deal at close quarters with such a violent temperament.

It was a partnership that promised to be a stormy one, he reflected as he came out again into the wintry morning sunshine of the High Street. But the promise of adventure was there also and that, together with the unaccustomed satisfaction of fresh hot food in his stomach, was enough to send his spirits soaring.

At the mouth of Beith's Wynd he paused to tuck the purse Macey had given him for Norton's burial safely inside his doublet, then stood for a moment looking down the High Street. As ever, it was busy and noisy as a fairground with the bargaining from the vendors' booths and the cries of street-sellers. Jamie, however, was a true son of the city, and happily absorbing the noise and bustle around him he considered where he might find Tod and the Cleek.

On such a fine morning, he calculated, there would almost certainly be a hunt in the park around the king's palace of Holyrood. Both Tod and Cleek were skilful at starting a deer. They loved a hunt and there was money to be earned in beating the woods. Holyrood was the most likely place to find them, and accordingly he set off eastwards towards the foot of the High Street.

Straddling the street here was the Netherbow Port, the easternmost gate in the city walls, with Holyrood a few hundred yards off and the street called Canongate connecting the two. If Tod and the Cleek has passed this way, Jamie reasoned, they would have been seen by the gatekeeper on duty at the Netherbow and he hailed the man with the question.

"Aye, they went through as soon as the gates were opened at dawn," the man shouted in reply. "The king was out early at the hunt this morning."

They would be miles off by this time in that case Jamie reflected as he set off at a rapid trot down the broad thoroughfare of the Canongate. To his surprise, however, he had run only a few yards when he saw the familiar figures of Tod and the Cleek advancing up the street towards him.

"Tod! Cleek!" he hailed delightedly, and quickened his pace to a run.

"What brought you so early from the hunt?" he questioned as they met, and the Cleek said disgustedly, "Well may you ask! That ever I should live to see King James stop the chase in full cry for such as the Earl of Huntly!"

"He had business to discuss with the king that would brook no delay, it seems," Tod explained.

"And the king stopped the chase?" Jamie asked in amazement.

"Aye, 'tis strange when you conside
the hunt," Tod agreed.

"There is naught strange about i
Cleek, "except that he fairly dotes on
George' he calls him — *dearest George*

With another snort of disgust a
thumped his cleek to the ground and
The other two fell into step and Tod,
said, "Well, well, Cleek. A king has few
ues those that he has." He turned f
scowling face to Jamie. "What news wi
asked.

"There is much to tell," Jamie sa
questions to ask, in especial touchin
Sempill — Colonel William Sempill."

Both Tod and the Cleek stopped dead
They looked at one another meaningly,
pointed with his stick to the sign han
ale house a few steps up the street.

"If that is the way things are," he sai
here at the Boar's Head. Lucky Finlays
there grooming a horse, and if both For
are concerned with your mysterious
will need his help."

"Why, what is there to connect them
in surprise.

"Liège," the Cleek said briefly. "
Liège."

No further word of explanation was
were settled in the taproom with ale-p
them and Tod had gone off to fetch L
yard. "What happened at Liège?" Jam
"and what have Lucky and Forbes to do

"They were all in the same regiment
the Spanish wars against the Netherla

On such a fine morning, he calculated, there would almost certainly be a hunt in the park around the king's palace of Holyrood. Both Tod and Cleek were skilful at starting a deer. They loved a hunt and there was money to be earned in beating the woods. Holyrood was the most likely place to find them, and accordingly he set off eastwards towards the foot of the High Street.

Straddling the street here was the Netherbow Port, the easternmost gate in the city walls, with Holyrood a few hundred yards off and the street called Canongate connecting the two. If Tod and the Cleek has passed this way, Jamie reasoned, they would have been seen by the gatekeeper on duty at the Netherbow and he hailed the man with the question.

"Aye, they went through as soon as the gates were opened at dawn," the man shouted in reply. "The king was out early at the hunt this morning."

They would be miles off by this time in that case Jamie reflected as he set off at a rapid trot down the broad thoroughfare of the Canongate. To his surprise, however, he had run only a few yards when he saw the familiar figures of Tod and the Cleek advancing up the street towards him.

"Tod! Cleek!" he hailed delightedly, and quickened his pace to a run.

"What brought you so early from the hunt?" he questioned as they met, and the Cleek said disgustedly, "Well may you ask! That ever I should live to see King James stop the chase in full cry for such as the Earl of Huntly!"

"He had business to discuss with the king that would brook no delay, it seems," Tod explained.

"And the king stopped the chase?" Jamie asked in amazement.

"Aye, 'tis strange when you consider his passion for the hunt," Tod agreed.

"There is naught strange about it," snapped the Cleek, "except that he fairly dotes on Huntly! 'Dearest George' he calls him — *dearest George!*"

With another snort of disgust at the words he thumped his cleek to the ground and moved off again. The other two fell into step and Tod, the peacemaker, said, "Well, well, Cleek. A king has few friends and values those that he has." He turned from the Cleek's scowling face to Jamie. "What news with you, boy?" he asked.

"There is much to tell," Jamie said, "and many questions to ask, in especial touching a man called Sempill — Colonel William Sempill."

Both Tod and the Cleek stopped dead in their tracks. They looked at one another meaningly, then the Cleek pointed with his stick to the sign hanging outside an ale house a few steps up the street.

"If that is the way things are," he said, "we will stop here at the Boar's Head. Lucky Finlayson is in the yard there grooming a horse, and if both Forbes and Sempill are concerned with your mysterious Englishman we will need his help."

"Why, what is there to connect them?" Jamie asked in surprise.

"Liège," the Cleek said briefly. "The Battle of Liège."

No further word of explanation was offered till they were settled in the taproom with ale-pots in front of them and Tod had gone off to fetch Lucky from the yard. "What happened at Liège?" Jamie asked then, "and what have Lucky and Forbes to do with Sempill?"

"They were all in the same regiment at the time of the Spanish wars against the Netherlands," the Cleek told him. "There were Scottish mercenaries fighting on the Netherlands side then, and it was one of these Scottish regiments that guarded the city of Liège. Lucky and Angus Mhor were foot-soldiers in it and John Forbes and his brother, Neil, were officers."

"And Sempill?" Jamie asked.

"He was their commanding officer," the Cleek replied.

"Aye, he was and all," Lucky's voice came from behind them. They turned to greet him, and lowering himself carefully on to the bench beside Jamie, Lucky propped his crutch in the corner and reached for the ale-pot the Cleek handed him.

"I have named the men of Liège to the boy," the Cleek said as he drank. "You and Angus Mhor and Forbes and Sempill. Now you must tell him what happened there."

"Simply done," Lucky said. He set down the empty ale-mug and looked at Jamie. "Sempill betrayed his own regiment to the Spaniards."

Incredulously Jamie looked from one to the other of the faces watching him, but the exclamation of horror on his lips was forestalled by Lucky.

"Wait till you know the facts," the one-legged man said, "and till you know the kind of man Sempill is. First and foremost, Jamie, he is a bonny fighter and a brave man. But he has a temper that would disgrace the devil himself, and he is a vengeful man that will not forgive an injury. Now," he settled the wounded leg more comfortably, "this is what happened.

"Liège, boy, was besieged by a Spanish army under the command of the Duke of Parma. Food was short and the governor of the city — who disliked Scotsmen for all that we were guarding his life — saw to it that our regiment came last in the sharing of what little there was. Matters grew very bad. For ten days we Scots had nothing to eat but grass and roots, and on the tenth night Sempill went to the governor's house to demand a share of the food that was left for his men.

"There was a quarrel, a fierce bitter quarrel. I was on guard duty at the governor's house that night, Jamie, and I heard it all, and I tell you he threw insults at Sempill that I knew could only be wiped out in blood. Sempill left the city that night, but before dawn the next morning he appeared again outside the city walls.

"He called up the password to the officer on garrison duty at the gate, and knowing his voice the officer opened to him. Sempill struck him down dead. Then, while the garrison was all in confusion over this happening, he pushed wide the gate and the troop of Spaniards in hiding outside the walls rushed through and overpowered the men on guard there.

"After that the way was clear. There was another, larger force of Spaniards waiting for this to happen. They poured into the city. Our men were taken by surprise, and in the half-dark they were slow to realize what had happened. The battle was short and bloody and Liège fell to the Spaniards."

He paused, looking down into his empty ale-mug while they all watched him tensely. At last he looked up. "That was when I lost this leg of mine," he said wryly, "and when Angus Mhor had the blow that lost him the power of speech. I have told you before, Jamie, how I saw John Forbes stand astride the Highlandman's body and fight off the three men that bore him down. But one thing I have not told you, though Tod and the Cleek know of it. The officer that Sempill slew at the gate that morning was Neil Forbes, brother to John Forbes, and with my own eyes I saw him kneeling by his murdered brother, weeping as he cradled the bloodied corpse in his arms and calling heaven to witness that he would hunt Sempill down and kill him."

"So now," the Cleek said, "you know the story of the men of Liège."

"'Tis a terrible tale," Jamie said thoughtfully, "and a terrible revenge to take on the governor."

"I told you he was a vengeful man," Lucky replied. "But he was still a good soldier, Jamie. He humbled himself to that purse-proud merchant that governed the city because his men were starving, and was treated like a dog for his pains. No one knew of it but me, and I dared not tell or the rest of the regiment would have slit my throat for taking Sempill's part. And even I, though I can understand the reasons for his revenge, cannot forgive the fact that he betrayed his own men to achieve it or that he was the means of putting us all into the hands of the man in black."

"*The man in black!*" Jamie exclaimed. "What had *he* to do with Liège?"

"He was the envoy who took over the city for the Duke of Parma," Lucky said grimly, "a cold, cruel-hearted devil of a man. I will not tell you of the way he treated the captured Scottish soldiers, Jamie. 'Tis not a story fit for any decent person's ears, but if ever evil stalked the earth it was in the shape of that man. Pray God he is not still alive to work his wickedness!"

With a sick feeling at the pit of his stomach Jamie said, "He *is* alive. He is passing by the name of M'sieur François d'Aquirre and he and Sempill are the two men I am seeking now on behalf of the Englishman, Macey."

"Well!" the Cleek exploded. "Well Jamie, you *have* got yourself into a pickle!"

With a sweep of his arm that sent the mugs clattering along the table he commanded, "Tell the wench to draw more ale, Tod. We will need to think this matter out."

Obediently Tod rose with the mugs, and when he had returned and set them down again Jamie began, "First I must tell you that Sempill is now a secret agent for the Spanish king."

"That I believe," the Cleek nodded. "There was a death sentence passed on him here in Scotland for the Liège treachery, and it is still in force. He would have no choice but to go over completely to the Spanish side — but go on with your story."

"The other thing I have discovered," Jamie went on, "is that the ballad-singer, Norton, was an agent for the English government."

"I knew it!" the Cleek exclaimed, but Tod hushed him with uplifted hand and Jamie was left to tell the rest of his story in peace. Purposely he omitted any mention of his attempt to bargain with Forbes for fencing lessons, but for the rest, he could judge by the faces of his listeners that they were convinced by Macey's arguments and approved his decision to help the Englishman.

"It puzzled me why Forbes should not disclose his interest in Sempill," he added after he had finished the main tale, "but now that Lucky has told the story of Liège, I can see why."

"Aye," Tod agreed. "Forbes means to kill Sempill and he knows that the Englishman will want him alive. He is not going to take the risk of losing his revenge by letting Macey know his purpose."

"It will be a matter of luck what happens," Lucky declared. "I am a great believer in luck myself and so was Sempill. He always used to say it was the one gift a soldier of fortune needed to have above all others, and he boasted, too, that he was a by-ordinar lucky man himself."

"Old wives tales!" the Cleek dismissed this contemptuously. He looked round at the others seeking assurance from them. "It is all agreed we stand by Jamie?" he demanded.

"Aye, the cause is just," Tod decided.

"Oh, I am all for backing him," Lucky said, "but the work is dangerous and he is only a lad, remember."

"I am not a bairn!" Jamie retorted. "I can take care of myself."

"Ye'll maybe can use a little help, though," Tod suggested in his gentle voice.

He flexed his big hands expressively and the Cleek added, "Or a wheen more knowledge than you have yourself! To begin with, there is something I learned from one of our fellows that has been working down in the city docks at Leith. A Netherlands ship has been standing at anchor in the harbour roads there for the past two days. She has discharged no cargo and yet there is no word of passengers aboard her either — and the Netherlands route, I would remind you, is the sea-route the Spaniards favour most.

"And another thing I know because I saw him myself going into the house of Paterson the tinsmith in the Upper Bow, is that a man called James Pringle is in Edinburgh. And Pringle, I'll have *you* know, has been servant to Sempill these many years past."

"I know him!" Lucky exclaimed. "He is Sempill's body-servant — a dark squat fellow he is, with a deep scar running right down one cheek from ear to mouth."

"The same," the Cleek nodded. "A quiet fellow, but cunning. He could be dangerous."

"And he could be a lead to Sempill," Jamie said. He rose with the words and drawing out the purse of money from his doublet he handed it to the Cleek. "I will have to report back to Mr Macey now," he said. "Will you and Tod make the arrangements I agreed on with him for Norton's burial and start the search for Sempill and d'Aquirre?"

"Aye, we"ll see Norton decently buried, lad," the Cleek assured him, "and as for the other two, the word for them will be all over the city within the hour. Meet us again at the Market Cross and you will see."

"And tell your Englishman we will set a watch on the house Pringle was seen to enter," Tod added. "You will have every caddie in Edinburgh behind you, Jamie, once the Cleek gives the word. Rely on us."

With this assurance ringing in his ears, Jamie left the ale house and made for Fisher's Close again and the house of Master Forbes.

"Mr Macey is out in the stable," Nan told him, "though what a gentleman like him can want in the stable, and Angus after having groomed his horse and all —"

Jamie ran off to the stable without waiting for her to finish though privately he was wondering himself what Macey could be finding to do there. He was saddling his horse, apparently, and he turned as Jamie's entrance blotted out the light from the stable door.

"You see this?" He indicated the animal. "I must have a horse ready to ride at all hours of the day and night, Jamie. That will be part of your task with me you understand? Now, I can see from your face that you have news."

"I have," Jamie said bluntly. "If you want Sempill alive you must reach him before Forbes does. Forbes has sworn to kill him."

Macey's face tightened with shock and anger. He moved to the stable door and looked out. The courtyard was deserted and he came back with the words, "We are safe from overhearing, but talk quietly. Tell me all you know."

In low rapid tones Jamie gave him an account of what he had learned from Lucky and told him of the arrangements that had been set in hand. Macey leant in thoughtful silence against the side of his mount's loose box for some time after he had finished speaking, and Jamie studied him curiously, wondering how he would deal with the dilemma of Forbes and Sempill.

"This alters your plans, does it not?" he asked eventually. "Will you leave the fencing master's house?"

"And have him suspect I know of his enmity to Sempill?" Macey asked. "No, I will play the cards off the top of the pack from now on — 'twill not be the first time! Besides, if I cannot take Sempill before he does, I can at least prevent them coming to close quarters if I stay here."

"You will not tell him about Pringle and the house in Upper Bow, then?"

"Indeed I will not!" Macey exclaimed, "and as soon as darkness falls we will take over the watch on it ourselves, for whatever is about to happen, it will be soon. Poor Norton was sure of that!"

"Till nightfall, then," Jamie agreed. "I will meet you at the mouth of Beith's Wynd, and until then I will join in the search with the rest of the caddies."

"Aye,'twill serve to keep you out of the way of Forbes's questioning," Macey said approvingly. "Meanwhile, I will ride to Leith and make further enquiries about this Netherlands ship."

"You know the way?" Jamie asked.

"In a general sense only," Macey admitted. "I feared

to bring Hertford's map in case I was captured on the road north and its presence showed me bound for Edinburgh. You had better refresh my memory."

"It is very simple," Jamie told him. "East down the High Street to the Netherbow Port in the city walls. Beyond this lies the street called Canongate with Leith Wynd running north-east off it and leading direct to Leith, two miles away."

"I have it clear now," Macey replied, "and here is a sum to cover the services of those employed in the watch for the Spanish agents."

Jamie took the coins he offered and regarded them with eyebrows raised in surprise.

"You continue generous, Mr Macey," he remarked, "and yet I have always heard that the English queen is careful with her coin!"

A little laugh escaped Macey. "Queen Elizabeth, God rest her, is thrifty indeed," he said, "but she would not have such an excellent espionage system if those who ruled it shared her views. There are ways and means of managing such things, Jamie."

And on the mutual chuckle that this comment evoked, they parted for the rest of the day.

5. The Man in Black

It was cold work waiting for Macey in the darkness of Beith's Wynd that night. Jamie hugged himself as he stood pressed against the wall, and shivering, he hoped that Mistress Marie would keep her promise to find him a warm garment and that Macey would not be long in appearing.

The watch passed by, lanterns swinging. Their voices calling the hour echoed back with hollow effect from the deserted street, and as they died away Macey appeared suddenly and silently beside him.

Jamie touched his arm. "This way," he whispered.

He moved out of the entry and turning right led the way up the High Street to where it opened out into the broad square of the Lawnmarket. The market booths, deserted for the night, crowded the square in an untidy huddle, and cautiously for fear of tripping he wove a way in and out of them towards the head of the Lawnmarket.

Here the street called the Upper Bow led almost due south off the High Street, and with another touch on Macey's arm Jamie indicated their change of direction. Halfway down the Bow he stopped suddenly, gripped Macey's arm, and pulling him sharply to the right turned into a narrow entry off the street. He whistled softly and two figures appeared immediately out of the shadows at the end of the entry.

They came noiselessly up to Jamie and Macey. "Pringle arrived just before dark," one of them muttered. "He is still in the house."

"Thanks, Cuddy," Jamie whispered, and the two caddies melted off into the darkness of the Bow.

"They have been watching since noon," Jamie whispered to Macey. "Paterson's house lies facing us on the other side of the street with the main door of it at the end of an entry like this one."

He squatted down with his back to the wall of the entry and Macey followed his example. There was little news to exchange for Macey had not been able to find out anything further about the Netherlands ship, and as their eyes became accustomed to the gloom they occupied themselves with studying the structure of Paterson's house.

It was a two-storeyed building with a gable end forming one side of the entry that led up to the main door. The gable was an ornamental affair projecting beyond the breadth of the roof and with its sides sloping up in a series of stone steps towards a fleur-de-lis carved on its peak. There was a dormer window in it that looked out on to the entry, and dormer windows also looked down from the wall that faced on to the Bow.

Beyond this, there was nothing to take up their attention and in spite of the cold Jamie felt himself dozing off as the time of waiting stretched out. A sudden movement from Macey jerked him wide awake.

"Footsteps," Macey muttered. "Listen!"

Jamie strained forward listening. The sound was faint but growing clearer. Someone was coming down the Bow towards them. Gently both he and Macey eased themselves to their feet and Macey's hand closed over the hilt of his sword.

The footsteps were cautious and rapid. They drew level with the entry, and on the opposite side of the street the dark figure of a man swung into Jamie's line of vision. He turned into the entry to Paterson's house and for a moment was swallowed up in the gloom of the narrow space. The door of the house swung open and a light shone out. The figure on the doorstep came momentarily into view as a tall man with hair gleaming golden-red in the shaft of light, then he vanished into the house and darkness reigned again with the closing of the door behind him.

"Sempill!" Jamie heard Macey breathe the word in unison with him.

"What now!" he whispered.

Macey was staring at the house opposite and impatiently Jamie waited for him to make a move. Still Macey waited and suddenly a light came up in the dormer window facing on to the entry. Immediately Macey turned to him.

"You know the structure of these houses," he whispered. "How can we overlook that window?"

"Follow me," Jamie whispered in reply, "and grip where I do."

He moved into the street, glanced up and down it to make sure they were unobserved, then darted over to the other side. In his mind's eye was a picture of the house on the other side of the entry from Paterson's. It had a flat-topped porch projecting over the ground floor that would give them their first hand-grip, and a stepped gable end like that on Paterson's house which would provide cover for observing the window opposite.

Macey was close on his heels. At the porch he stopped and bent over, hands clasping his knees. Macey's foot pressed on to his spine, then his weight lifted abruptly as he jumped. A thud and a scrabble told of his gaining the roof of the porch. Jamie straightened up and Macey's voice came from above. "Grasp this now!" He jumped for the sword-belt that came snaking down from above him. He grasped it and his feet were swung out from under him as Macey took the strain, then he was up and scrambling back on to his feet on the flat roof.

Once again he took the lead, using the method of roof-climbing that the boys of Edinburgh were accustomed to play as a game. Lying on his side and gaining leverage from his feet pushing against the projecting part of the gable end he pulled himself hand over hand up the roof. Twice he slipped and felt his feet strike Macey's head below but the other made no sound.

He reached the ridge that marked the end of the second storey and lifted himself to lie full-length along it keeping his head down behind the decorative stone carving that marked the peak of the gable. Macey lay at right angles to him down the length of the roof and concealed by the stepped edge of the gable-wall. Their heads were almost touching.

"Now!" he whispered, and both raised their heads to peer over the gable.

The lit room was four feet from them in distance, several feet below them, and slightly to their right. The light in it came from a candle on the table in the middle of the room. Two men stood by the table, a dark squat man dressed like a servant and with a deep scar running down one cheek, and a tall man elegantly clad, with hair and beard of golden-red.

It was Sempill and Pringle without a doubt, but even the discovery of these two was over-shadowed by the sight of the small leather valise that lay on the table between them. It was open, and it was filled with coins that winked and glittered in the candlelight in a solid golden mass.

As Jamie watched in amazement, Sempill plunged his hands into the bag. The mass of gold broke and shifted in a myriad points of light as he scooped out a double handful of the coins. He spread them out, counted them, and several more little columns of gold went to join those already counted out on to the table.

"I did not think there was so much gold in the world!" he whispered to Macey.

"Spanish gold!" the Englishman muttered angrily. "Now I know that —" He stopped short as Pringle turned to leave the room and they waited in silence to see what would happen next.

Sempill continued to count out the money. He was smiling to himself and Jamie watched him, fascinated by his swashbuckling appearance and extraordinary occupation.

Suddenly the utter silence of the street was startled by the sound of approaching footsteps. Jamie froze, waiting for the steps to pass. They drew level with Paterson's house, but instead of passing it grew louder as the newcomer came up the entry below them. Faint sounds below told of the door opening and closing again.

Cautiously Jamie allowed a few seconds to pass before he raised his head again. In the room opposite Sempill had turned towards the door, head inclined as he listened. The seconds crept by, then the door opened and Pringle came back into the room. A man stood behind him in the doorway, a tall thin man dressed from head to foot in unrelieved black.

His lips moved as he said something to Sempill and with a sharp gesture of his arm indicated the window. Sempill shrugged, and in obedience to the gesture Pringle crossed the room and pulled the shutters closed.

"Quickly, Jamie!" Macey's voice came immediately. "We must get down from here."

He began slithering down. Jamie followed, his mind a turmoil of questions, but when they reached the ground again Macey gave him no opportunity to talk.

"This chance may never come my way again," he said rapidly. "Sempill and d'Aquirre together *and* the gold for their schemes! But I cannot hope to capture them without the help of Forbes and Angus Mhor. I am going now to fetch them and I will try to convince Forbes that Sempill must be taken alive. You will stay here on watch, and if they leave the house before I can return follow them and mark where they go. And at all costs, keep the gold in sight!"

Without waiting for a reply he was off, running lightly on his toes, and Jamie moved back into the entry opposite Paterson's house. Looming in his mind as he squatted again was the question of how long it would take Macey to rouse Forbes and Angus Mhor and return to the Bow. The half of an hour at the soonest, he thought, if Forbes came without question, but if he stopped to dispute with Macey there was no telling when they would appear.

He settled to wait, his eyes firmly fixed on the line of light that showed under the shutters. A quarter of an hour went by. The light vanished suddenly, and obeying the impulse that leapt into his mind he crossed the street quickly and ran up to the door of Paterson's house. He huddled down on the doorstep, his head on his knees. Footsteps sounded faintly from behind the closed door then it swung open and two men emerged, almost falling over his crouched form.

"What the devil —!" one of them exploded.

Jamie jumped to his feet, cringing away from them. "Your pardon, gentle sirs," he whined. "I was seeking a place to sleep and ventured to use the cover of your doorway. Do not charge me to the magistrates, I beg you!"

He backed away down the entry, keeping up his beggar's whining and one of them said impatiently, "Come, 'tis only a beggar-boy. There's no harm done!"

They moved forward to where he crouched against the wall of the house, carefully turning their heads away from his vision as they passed him. The light from the opening doorway, however, had shown Jamie what he had hoped to find out. It was Sempill and the man in black who had emerged from the house, but it was the latter who was now in charge of the valise full of gold.

Exultant at the success of his ruse he waited till they were far enough ahead for him to follow them unobserved, and so preoccupied was he with this that he failed to observe the now-darkened doorway opening quietly again. Nor did he notice, as he stepped quietly up the Bow in pursuit of the first two, that Pringle was following him as unobtrusively as he followed Sempill and d'Aquirre.

At the head of the Bow the two men paused before, as he had feared they would, they parted company. Sempill moved off eastwards down the High Street, keeping well in the shadow of the house fronts. Valise in hand, the man in black stepped out to cross the Lawnmarket, and keeping as close as he dared Jamie followed his progress in and out of the huddle of booths. Sempill was well and truly lost now, he thought in some dismay as he slipped from cover to cover, but Macey's instructions had been to keep the gold in sight at all costs and it was inconceivable that it could have been left behind in the tin-smith's house. It must be in the valise gripped in d'Aquirre's hand now.

They reached the north side of the Lawnmarket and the man in black turned into an entry leading off it. It was almost pitch-black in this narrow space and Jamie closed the gap between them as much as he dared. The man in black turned left off the entry. A few yards on he turned right, then left again into another narrow entrance, and Jamie's heart sank. These old buildings north of the High Street were connected by an absolute maze of narrow passages such as those they had already traversed and he knew them well enough to realize it would be almost impossible to follow d'Aquirre through them without being observed.

The man in black seemed familiar, also, with the maze. He walked rapidly with long, almost soundless strides, and the pattern of his twistings and turnings grew more and more complicated. There was no possible way of judging his destination from it except that the general direction of his route continued to be northerly.

They would soon be out on the banks of the Nor Loch at this rate, Jamie thought. A cat darting from a doorway ran squalling between his legs. He stumbled and almost fell and recovered his balance only just in time to see the figure of the man in black turning down yet another opening.

A panic fear that he had lost his quarry at last made Jamie throw caution aside. He rushed forward and peered down the entry. Nothing moved in the darkness ahead but in this passage, he knew, there were no openings leading off to left or right. There was only an exit at the further end leading almost on to the shores of the Nor Loch, and to vanish so quickly, therefore, the man in black must have run down the passageway and left it by this exit.

The only other alternative, Jamie thought with a sudden shiver of fear, was that all the twists and turns d'Aquirre had taken were part of a deliberate plan that showed he knew he was being followed. And having failed to throw off his pursuer he was waiting, hidden somewhere in that narrow channel of darkness, ready to leap out and kill.

"*If ever evil stalked the earth it was in the shape of that man.*"

Lucky's sombre words sounded again in his ears but with an effort of will he shrugged them off. He was hardened enough in bone and sinew to hold his own in the fierce life of the streets, he thought grimly, and the man in black would not have matters entirely his own way in a struggle.

He started off down the passage, crouched, his hands held ready in front of him. Nothing moved in the darkness ahead. There was no sound but his own soft footsteps. Step by careful step, he advanced. The passage began to lighten with the dim reflection from the waters of the Nor Loch ahead. If the man in black was there he had miscalculated his position. Any movement on his part now would be seen against that pallid light.

It was with a feeling of anticlimax that he reached the end of the passage safely. His feet sank into mud and ahead of him lay the grey ghostly waters of the loch. He moved forward, casting this way and that for any sign of life but the shore of the loch was utterly deserted. The man in black had escaped him.

With a dismal sense of failure weighing him down, Jamie turned away and took a direct route south back to the High Street. As he walked he debated whether he should return to the house in the Bow or whether it would be better to go to Forbes's house, but in the end he was saved the necessity of making a decision. The way he chose brought him out at a point slightly above Beith's Wynd, and as he emerged into the street he heard footsteps and voices.

He waited, keeping back into the shadows till the

men he had heard drew near enough to be identified. They were Macey, Forbes, and Angus Mhor, and as soon as he realized this he stepped forward and hailed them softly. They crowded round him, Forbes and Macey questioning simultaneously. Macey received his story in silence but Forbes exclaimed violently,

"So we have nothing to show for the night's work! The gold is gone and the villains vanished before we can reach them, and the boy did not even manage to keep track of one of them!"

"At least we know who has the gold now," Macey defended him. "Be fair to the boy, Forbes. It was not an easy assignment."

"Aye well, maybe you are right," Forbes grumbled. "Well, let's to bed. There is nothing to be gained from staying here."

"Come, cheer up Jamie. This is only the first round," Macey said kindly. He laid his hand on Jamie's shoulder and added reassuringly, "If we have not gained anything tonight, at least we are not worse off than we were before!"

They moved off in a body, unaware of the squat dark man lurking in the shadows behind them or of the ironical smile that spread across his scarred face as he listened to these words.

6. *Norton's Cloak*

There was a council of war at Forbes's house early next morning. It was held in Mistress Marie's private parlour and to Jamie's disapproval, when he arrived there, he found it included Mistress Marie herself.

"Ah, Jamie," she said graciously, "we are just about to discuss what is to happen next now that I know my father is once more in pursuit of this man Sempill."

"You drew the knowledge from me with your pretty ways, you minx!" Forbes growled.

"You know very well, Papa," she retorted "that I promised Maman before she died that I would try to stop you from running into trouble over Colonel Sempill. Uncle Neil is dead, Papa. What difference will it make to him if you do kill Sempill in revenge?"

"Neil was murdered!" Forbes roared. "Stay out of this, miss, do you hear! My brother was murdered and I will revenge him!"

"You see?" She shrugged expressively and turned to Macey. "This wicked temper of my father's — it will be the ruin of him."

"He is right in one respect," Macey said gravely. "It is dangerous work — the more so since it crosses the business in which I am engaged. You *should* stay out of it."

"I am a soldier's daughter," she said composedly, "and I am no stranger to siege and battle. I am not afraid of danger, M'sieu Macey."

It was bravely spoken and Jamie's disapproval of her presence in the council melted with the words. Macey, however, was still cautious.

"If your father has told you also of my business you

will know that his purpose with Sempill is at odds with mine," he said warily.

"He has kept nothing from me," she said, "and it is just because you wish to take Sempill alive that I wish to help you. I want to save my father from himself."

"Forbes, what do you say?" Macey appealed, but the fencing master was adamant.

"You cannot move me," he said grimly. "I will help you to track down both Sempill and d'Aquirre because I passed my word to do so, but if you wish to take Sempill alive you must reach him before I do. That is my final word, Macey."

"Then I regret I must leave your house and pursue my search alone," Macey said.

"No!" Forbes leapt to his feet and advanced on the Englishman with the exclamation. "You are too valuable an ally for me to lose now, Macey. Either we work together on this or I will have you cried abroad for an English spy!"

Marie also jumped to her feet with a cry of protest at her father's words. Jamie joined his voice to hers, but Macey silenced them both with a gesture.

"Very well, Forbes," he said calmly. "You hold the ace at present, but remember that I am pledged to bring Sempill in for questioning and honour may prove the trump card in the end."

"Well spoken!" Jamie applauded involuntarily.

But Marie exclaimed, "Oh, pray let us stop this foolish quarrelling and talk sensibly! M'sieu Macey, tell us what you think about the bag of gold you saw."

"I can only hazard a guess," Macey shrugged. "The gold was most likely brought from Spain by Sempill aboard the Netherlands ship now at Leith, and delivered to d'Aquirre for the purpose on which they are both engaged."

"One thing is certain," Forbes commented gloomily. "They will be well warned by this time that we raided the house in the Bow after they left it last night. They will not use it as a rendezvous again."

"That line of enquiry is closed to us," Macey agreed. "All we can do now is to take up the thread again from the occasion that Norton was killed — the gathering of Catholic nobility at the de Guise palace."

"And how will you do that?" Marie asked.

"I shall present myself at Court all fashionably attired and mingle with the gilded gossips of Holyrood," Macey replied smilingly. "I have come prepared against the possibility of such a move with letters of introduction from Queen Elizabeth commending her well-beloved esquire, Roger Macey, to the good graces of her dear cousin James, King of Scots."

"Foresight indeed!" Forbes commented.

Macey bowed an acknowledgement. "You, good Master Forbes, will be my escort," he continued, "and introduce me to all the pretty fighting gentlemen such as the Earl of Huntly and his friends of the night of the twenty-fourth of January."

"Aye, talk of arms will bring out talk of battles," Forbes said thoughtfully, "battles past, present — and still to come!"

"A chance word here, a chance word there — who knows what information we may uncover," Macey agreed. He turned to Jamie. "Now your part, boy. A day and night watch must be kept on that ship at Leith. And the part of the city where d'Aquirre vanished — that must be thoroughly searched. All the gates into the city must be watched, change-house ostlers questioned over any hire of horses to the south, and a special watch kept for the circulation of any

Spanish gold currency. All this to be done till I give the word to abandon the search."

With a wave of the hand that dismissed Jamie from the council he turned to the other two. Jamie turned to go, but at the doorway of the room he paused. He had failed to keep d'Aquirre in sight, it was true, but he *had* found Sempill and Forbes *had* agreed to discuss the subject of fencing lessons if he did so. The reminder trembled on the tip of his tongue but before he could say anything Macey and Forbes were deep in conversation and the opportunity to speak was gone.

He would not so lightly let another one pass by, he vowed as he made his way to the Market Cross. The memory of Macey's instinctive reach for his sword at the sound of Sempill's footsteps the previous night recurred to him, and his determination grew. With a sword at his side, he thought, and the skill in his arm to use it, he would be able to ride abroad as Macey did, the whole world of adventure open to him and himself a match for any man in it!

The sight of the Cleek's wrinkled face peering at him from the steps of the Market Cross brought him back to earth.

"Well Jamie, what's to do?" the old man enquired.

"We are to keep the watch up," Jamie told him, and went on to give Macey's instructions in detail. At the mention of the watch for Spanish gold coins the Cleek said:

"George Heriot, the king's jeweller, is the man for that. They say he can tell every piece of gold in the city as well as a shepherd can tell his sheep. I will speak to him, Jamie — he has always a kind word for old Cleek."

"Here comes Tod," Jamie remarked.

"Aye, and Cuddy and Daddler, the two that watched

at Paterson's, with him. Now we can put the word round. You will be run off your legs before the day is out, Jamie."

The Cleek was as good as his word. Before the supper hour struck that evening Jamie had traversed miles of streets and spoken to hundreds of people, but despite the closeness of the search the day's results were meagre. Several people in the vicinity of Blair's Close claimed to have seen a man of d'Aquirre's build at some time in the past weeks, but as each sighting had been in the hours of darkness none could swear to his description.

As for the Netherlands ship, a fisherman at Leith had told Cuddy and Daddler of seeing a boat rowed out to it early that morning. The two caddies had persuaded the man to take them out in his boat on a round trip of the ship, only to retire hastily at the captain's threat to stand clear of it or he would blow them out of the water.

"But he was a Spaniard, that I'll swear to," Cuddy told Jamie. "He had all the looks of a Don and the queer way of talking they have."

With this for his only information Jamie returned to Forbes's house and gratefully fell to on the supper Nan set out in the kitchen for himself and Angus Mhor.

"You are to go to Mistress Marie when you have eaten," Nan told him. "She has that cloak she promised you."

So she *has* remembered, Jamie thought, and as soon as supper was finished he ran upstairs and knocked on the parlour door.

"Jamie?" Marie's voice came from within. "Come in. I have something for you."

As Jamie pushed open the door she came towards him, smiling, a blue woollen cloak draped over her arm. "I had forgotten this was here till Nan reminded me," she said. "It belonged to that poor fellow, Norton, but you might as well have it now, Jamie."

"*Norton's* cloak?" Jamie asked.

"Yes, he left it here that night he called to see papa — the night he was murdered by those wicked men, you remember? Poor man, he must have been very upset to forget his cloak."

Slowly Jamie took the cloak from her outstretched hand. Had Norton been upset that night? It seemed strange that a man who went boldly alone to such a rendezvous should have forgotten his cloak out of nervousness.

Macey had searched the dead man's clothes, he remembered. At the time it had seemed a strange thing for a man to do to his dead friend, but he had realized since then that Macey had hoped to find a message of some kind. There was no pocket in the cloak, however, not even a lining to conceal such a message. Still moving slowly he put the cloak on, fastened the clasp at the neck and stood staring at Mistress Marie.

"Why, Jamie," she exclaimed, "it gives you quite an air!"

Still Jamie stared at her without speaking and she said impatiently, "Come, are you not pleased to have such a fine warm cloak to wear?"

Between stiff lips he managed to say, "The collar is stiff — it scratches my neck."

"Oh!" she gasped. "You do not deserve it. You are wickedly ungrateful!"

The paralysis that held Jamie suddenly vanished. With a violent movement he snatched off the cloak. "Quick! A pair of sewing scissors!" he demanded.

Without waiting for permission he snatched up a little pair of silver scissors lying beside a work-box on the table. With clumsy rapidity he slashed at the stitching that held the folds of the broad collar in place. Marie watched him, too astonished to speak at first, but as the double fold of the collar began to open out under the scissors she cried out in protest.

Ignoring her, Jamie threw down the scissors and tore at the collar with his hands. It ripped apart and a stiffly-folded sheet of paper dropped from it on to the floor. He pounced on it and carefully opened it out, only to stand gazing uncomprehendingly at what he saw.

"What is it? What have you found?" Marie demanded.

Jamie handed the paper to her. "I cannot read — tell me what it says," he said desperately. "It *must* be important or Norton would not have hidden it in the cloak."

Marie looked up from the paper, frowning. "I think it *is* important," she said slowly. "It is a cipher of some kind that is written here."

"Then read it!" Jamie cried. "You have book learning — you must know what it says!"

"You foolish boy!" she said sharply. "Book learning does not mean that one can read a thing like this. It is a code, a secret code for sending hidden messages. No one can read it — unless —" She stopped, her face lighting up suddenly at the sound of footsteps outside the door. It opened, and with the paper held out in her hand she finished, "— unless, perhaps, M'sieu Macey knows the secret."

"What's this? You are talking of me?" Macey's voice was jovial as he came into the room with Forbes behind him, both men evidently in high good humour. The paper in Marie's outstretched hand and the anxious faces of herself and Jamie quieted them abruptly.

"A secret cypher, M'sieu Macey," Marie said quietly.

"Jamie found it hidden in the collar of an old cloak left here by your friend, Norton."

Macey took the paper from her and without a word went over to her writing desk and drew a clean sheet of parchment and a quill towards him. The other three moved over to the desk, crowding together to look over his shoulder as he began to write.

"It is the alphabet of a cypher," Forbes said in a low voice to Marie. "Look there, see how it is set out with numbers that equal each letter in the alphabet. See, an A is equal to the figure 10. B has the value of 49 or 70, D is equal to either a 72 or a 48, and E to 20 or 17 — and so on."

"There is a message there too, is there not?" Marie whispered. "There, at the foot of the paper where the numbers are all grouped together."

"Aye, he is working to translate it," Forbes answered.

The whispered conversation made no sense to Jamie. Bewildered and suddenly acutely aware of the handicap of ignorance he stared at the columns of numerals and letters, and a determination to be rid of such a handicap grew in him with every passing moment.

Macey swung round in his chair at last. The paper he had written on shook slightly in his hand, but his voice was firm as he said, "This is the message Norton left for me." Reading from the paper, he went on,

"Roger: Huntly, Errol, Crawford, and Hamilton are the men you seek, and possibly one other whose name I have not yet learned though I think that — unlike these four — he may be of the Protestant faith. Huntly is the chief of them and they are in correspondence with King Philip of Spain. To what purpose I know not yet, but having managed to obtain the alphabet of the code they

use for their Spanish letters I have left it hidden here in my cloak for you. Tonight may uncover more, but I have stretched my luck to the limit, and if I do not return from the rendezvous I leave it to you to foil their plans. But make haste, Roger. I fear that time is short."

"It is signed, '*Yours with affection, Ralph*,'" Macey finished.

He turned from them and leaned his elbow on the writing desk, his hand to his brow as if to shade his eyes. No one spoke for several minutes.

"That is all? No further word?" Forbes asked at last.

"Yes, he wrote one more thing." Macey rose to his feet and faced them with the words. "At the foot of his letter are the words, '*God save the Queen!*'"

He looked at them each now, one by one, as if willing them to his obedience. "Elizabeth, by the grace of God, is Queen of England," he said intensely, "and so she shall remain. Ralph Norton died to ensure this, and I, Roger Macey, pledged also to her service, do swear now before you all that I will finish his task."

Standing before them so, pale-faced, his eyes shining with an unnatural brilliance, he looked like a man in the grip of a fever. Jamie watched him, fascinated, unable to look away from the piercing stare of his eyes. Forbes was equally held, and it was left to Marie to break the spell.

"You are overwrought, M'sieu Macey," she said quietly.

With light steps she went over to a cupboard in the wall and brought back a tray with a decanter of wine and glasses on it. She poured a glassful and handed it to Macey, and then filling another two she served her father and Jamie. Last of all she poured wine for herself, and noting the order of serving, it occurred to Jamie how far she had moved in a single day from her opposition to the equal status accorded him by her father and Macey.

"To a brave man," she said, raising her glass, "and to the success of the venture he began."

They drained the wine. The colour came back into Macey's face and speaking once more in his normal voice he said, "Mistress Marie, I have a plan that may help us and your father is agreeable to it if you are willing to assist me."

"More than ever now," she answered. "What is it that you wish me to do?"

"Master Forbes and I have found out something at Court that seems highly significant," Macey told her. "The king, as you know, has a personal guard of trusted men always about him, but in the last few weeks every single man in that bodyguard has been quietly dismissed his post. The Earl of Huntly has seen to their replacement, and the king's entire bodyguard now is composed of Huntly's retainers."

He paused as if to make sure they had grasped what he said and then continued, "Norton has uncovered that Huntly is the chief conspirator and so this packing of the king's bodyguard with his own men can mean only one thing. He intends to seize the person of the king to further his plots with the Spaniards."

"But surely," Marie protested, "you have only to show Norton's letter to the king and explain this to him for him to clap the wicked Earl up in gaol?"

"'Twould be not the slightest use, Mistress Marie," Jamie said. "He so dotes on Huntly that the Earl can do nothing wrong in his eyes."

"The boy is right, Marie," Forbes said. "He would never believe Macey's word against that of Huntly's."

"But the letter," Marie insisted, "it is all written in the letter!"

"The king would not accept a letter in code from an English agent as proof of Huntly's guilt," Macey told her. "We need more than that, Mistress Marie. We need the Spanish Letters themselves."

"And that is where you can play a part, my dear," Forbes said. "The Countess of Huntly is a foolish, petted girl full of imagined ailments, and I have had a long talk with her today about my daughter's skill in curing the migraine and all her other pretended ills. She is very eager for you to come to her house in the Canongate and try some of your receipts on her."

"In other words," Macey said bluntly, "your father is agreeable that you should enter the Countess's household as a spy, your mission to be to find out how and where I can lay hands on the Spanish Letters."

"On one condition, Macey," Forbes reminded him. Turning again to Marie he went on, "I will let you enter Huntly House only if Angus Mhor goes with you and stays always within call. Are you willing to do this, my dear?"

"Of course, Papa," she said readily. "A foolish girl like this young Countess, she will talk freely I am sure, and perhaps I will learn much information from her."

"Are you not afraid?" Forbes asked gently.

"Afraid!" Marie cried. With a sudden clap of her hands and a laugh that startled them all she jumped to her feet and pirouetted round the room. Her gaiety was so infectious that within seconds they were all laughing with her. "I am like you Papa!" she cried through their laughter. "Danger makes me happy!"

"Run, boy! Run and fetch Angus Mhor!" Forbes shouted. "Let him see the wild bird he has to guard this time!"

With wings on his heels, Jamie flew down the stairs from the parlour. "*Now! Now!*" ran feverishly through his mind. Now was the time to bring Forbes back to his promise of a bargain over Sempill — now while the discovery of Norton's message was fresh and the promise of action drew near for them all. This very night he would pin Master Forbes down to the promise of a lesson!

Bursting into the kitchen where Angus Mhor sat whittling at a piece of wood with his dirk, he shouted:

"You are wanted upstairs, Angus! Come quickly!"

The dumb giant heaved himself to his feet and his hand went questioningly to the massive sword leaning against the chimney-pieces.

"Aye, buckle it on," Jamie said exultantly. "There is work on hand for swords now, Angus — mine maybe, as well as yours!"

7. *A Sword for Jamie*

It proved easier to gain Forbes's consent than he had expected. He waited till the fencing master broke away from the group to pour more wine for himself, and followed him across the room. Macey, Marie, and Angus Mhor were too absorbed to heed him, but he kept his voice low, nevertheless, for fear of another refusal.

The fencing master put down his glass, a broad smile overspreading his face. "I knew you were unruly," he said. "I see now you are also determined. But you have kept your side of the bargain. Come with me."

He led the way from the parlour, down the stairs and along the passage that led to the *salle d'armes*.

"First we must see if you are worth a lesson," he commented.

He took down a pair of foils and handed one to Jamie. "On your mark, boy," he said briskly. Taking up position himself, he brought his blade to the salute.

Jamie copied the action. His hand, sweating with nervousness, slipped on the hilt and the slender blade quivered in a blur of silver light. The stance, the passes Lucky had taught him flashed through his mind.

"*En garde!*" Forbes called, and Jamie's mind went blank. The next thing he knew the foil was flying out of his hand and he was looking along the arc of the fencing master's blade bent upwards from its point against his chest. He leapt back, recovered his foil in a scrambling rush and bore down on Forbes. For the space of a dozen strokes he held his own then once more his blade went flying, but this time Forbes put his foot on it before he could reach it.

"Now, Jamie," he said pleasantly, "calm yourself and listen to me. Be angry before you fight, be angry when you have finished. But never, as you did just now, let anger rule you while the sword is in your hand. It takes brains to be a swordsman, Jamie, and an angry man cannot fight well because he cannot think well. Now once again, slowly from the *en garde* and making each stroke from the count I give."

Once again the salute and the *en garde*, and the lesson began in earnest. Jamie's brain was clear now. Alert, he followed the count, moving with precision he corrected his stance to order as Forbes's voice marked each lunge, parry, and riposte.

It was exhilarating to feel the blade coming more and more under his control but at the end of half an hour he was sweating freely and his right wrist was aching.

"Rest now," Forbes called. He reached out his hand for the other foil and anxiously Jamie awaited his verdict. The fencing master's face was inscrutable.

"What weapon have you used for practice?" he asked.

"Any one at all I could lay hands on," Jamie confessed.

"And for how long?"

"For three years — ever since I was twelve years old."

"And it was Lucky who taught you the strokes." Forbes weighed the foils thoughtfully in his hands. "H'mmm. That maybe accounts for that chopping stroke you have developed. You will have to avoid that with the rapier, Jamie. 'Tis more properly a sabre stroke."

"Does that mean you will teach me, sir?" Jamie asked, and could hear his voice trembling on the words.

"You have a quick eye — a very quick eye and a good sense of timing," Forbes said, "but you are still lunging beyond your reach. Sword-play is a question of balance, Jamie. You must not lunge so far that the angle of the left shoulder ceases to balance that of the right knee. Keep the centre of your balance under control and you will be able to calm that thrashing arm of yours and manipulate the blade — as you should — from the wrist."

"But — you have not said —" Jamie stammered.

"The hour before breakfast tomorrow. An hour again before noon," Forbes interrupted him. "And if you are still on your feet, an hour again before supper."

He hung up the foils and strode to the door. "And if you keep me waiting for the lessons I will whip you!" he shouted over his shoulder, and was gone, leaving Jamie speechless.

Still hardly able to believe that he had heard correctly he retired to the kitchen for the night, and lying there on his truckle bed he considered Forbes's astounding offer. Astounding it assuredly was. The fencing master was known to be generous in all other matters, but he charged a justifiably high fee for his skill and when finally he had absorbed the extent of his good fortune Jamie hardly knew whether to be elated or dismayed at the challenge it offered.

The mixture of emotions pursued him into sleep, troubling his dreams with fantastic visions of flashing swords and phantom adversaries that mocked and vanished when he tried to pin them down in combat. But despite his troubled night he woke refreshed and eager for the first lesson of the day. Forbes was hard on his heels as he entered the *salle d'armes* and he drove at the lesson then — as Jamie was to discover he would do at all the subsequent ones — with an energy and intensity that surpassed all expectation. It seemed that having undertaken to teach Jamie he was determined to give of his utmost, with the result that by the end of his third day of careful coaching Jamie's worst faults had been corrected and he had begun to develop a certain degree of skill and style.

No further news of Sempill or d'Aquirre came to distract his concentration on Forbes's instructions. The Netherlands ship continued to ride at anchor with no indication of why she should be there at Leith. Macey remained shut in his room practising hour after hour to make himself fluent in the cypher, and Heriot the jeweller swore there was no Spanish gold in circulation in the city. The only person with any fresh news was Marie and even she had nothing to report but gossip.

"This poor Countess," she told them, "she is lonely, you understand. Why, she has been married only a year and yet she scarcely sees her husband! She has nothing to do but talk for hours about her migraine and all her other troubles."

"You must keep her talking about Huntly," Macey said at one of their councils. "Sooner or later she will tell you something important about him."

It was on the fourth day after the cypher was found — the seventh since Macey had arrived in Edinburgh — that two further events of importance happened, the first of which was, for Jamie, the most memorable event of his life.

Macey had come down to the *salle d'armes* to watch Jamie and Forbes at work. It was the first time he had appeared there since the tuition began, and Forbes said casually to him:

"Take a turn on the floor with the boy, Macey, and tell me what you think of his progress."

Jamie took off his doublet and laid it beside the blue

woollen cloak, its collar now mended again by Mistress Marie. Macey also stripped for action and they faced one another at the salute. For a moment Jamie's confidence wavered at the sight of Macey's superior height and lithe build, but the feeling vanished at the first touch of steel on steel. Quickly he found the other's measure, and fighting with all the skill and coolness Forbes had taught him he succeeded in achieving a hit before Macey struck back in a determined attack that pressed his guard open and forced him to yield the encounter.

Macey advanced on him with outstretched hand. "By the lord Harry," he said warmly, "Forbes has made a swordsman out of you, Jamie!"

"He had three years of good experience and hard practice behind him," Forbes said. "I have only put a polish on what was there already — but I had my reasons, all the same."

Turning to Jamie he commanded, "Fetch me that sword-belt from over yonder."

Jamie took the sword-belt with its weapon in the scabbard from the hook that Forbes indicated and brought it to him. "Put it on," Forbes said, and wonderingly, Jamie obeyed. Forbes laid a hand on his shoulder. "Wear it — it is yours," he said, "for two reasons, Jamie. First, for my daughter's safety. All who are concerned in this business in which she has taken a hand must be fit to guard her if the need arises. And second, because you have proved yourself brave and skilful enough to deserve such a weapon."

Overwhelmed, Jamie tried to speak but the utterance choked in his throat and he had only just succeeded in stammering out his thanks when Marie came flying into the room in a rush of skirts and high heels pattering over the floor.

"It has happened!" she cried. "Papa, M'sieu Macey, Jamie! It has happened at last!"

They crowded round her questioning eagerly, and still breathless from her run, Marie poured out her news.

"All day," she said, "the Countess has been complaining how the Earl neglects her. So I encourage her, you understand, and then she tells me that she is angry because tonight he will be at home to a gathering of his friends, but she is not invited because it is all men and they are going to talk business. '*It is politics, too,*' she says, '*because that horrid M'sieur d'Aquirre will be there with his grim face and his gloomy black clothes!*'"

"At last!" Macey exclaimed. "But we must, we *must* find out what goes on at that meeting!"

"Calm yourself, M'sieu Macey," Marie said. "I know how it can be done. Papa, give me a piece of that chalk you use for marking the floor."

Forbes handed her the chalk and she knelt down, talking rapidly as she sketched a diagram on the floor. "Here is Huntly House, see, standing on the right-hand side of the Canongate as you go down to Holyrood. Here, on the first floor, is the salon where the meeting will be held. It faces on to the Canongate and is windowed on that side. Here is one side wall of that room, and as you can see, it is also the outside wall of one side of the house. There is only one window in this side wall and that is the window of a little turret that projects from the outside wall and which houses a prayer closet leading off the room."

"A prayer closet?" Macey interrupted.

"Yes, yes, a common structure in Edinburgh houses," Forbes said impatiently. "'Tis a little space the size of a cupboard built on to the general structure of a room and set aside for the private devotions of the master of the house. Proceed, Marie."

"There is a heavy screen of open-carved wood separating the prayer closet from the salon," Marie continued. "It is solid wood at the foot and anyone crouched behind it would be invisible to the people in the room. But he would be able to hear everything that was said, and if he was cautious, to observe everything that was done."

"Can the prayer closet be entered without going through the house?" Macey demanded.

"Yes, if you go through an archway at that side you will find yourself in a broad passageway leading to the stables," she told him, "and the turret window looks down on to this passage. There is a *prie-dieu* of solid stone mortared on to the floor of the prayer closet. It would support the weight of anyone agile enough to climb up a rope attached to it and dropped through the turret window. Then, when the meeting is finished, I can slip into the prayer closet, untie the rope and take it back to my room, and no one but ourselves will ever know the meeting has been overlooked."

Macey looked at her with open admiration. "You have thought of everything," he said.

"I have also thought of a good excuse for going back now to tie the rope in position," she replied smilingly. "I was so sympathetic, you see, that the Countess insisted I should stay overnight at Huntly House so that I can keep her company while her husband neglects her for this meeting! But first I had to come and tell you about it and obtain the rope and so I said I must go to ask permission to stay from home for the night. Angus came with me and he is away now fetching the rope from the stable."

"One strong enough to bear my weight, I trust!"

Macey said, smiling in reply, and was stunned into silence by the answer.

"But the window is too small for *you* to enter, M'sieu Macey."

Quickly, before he could draw breath to argue, Jamie asked, "Will it take me, Mistress Marie?"

"Why yes, that is why I thought of the plan," she said. "The window is just wide enough for you to enter, but so narrow that they may overlook it as a means of entry."

"I told you, Macey," Forbes said, grinning at his discomfiture. "A boy can enter places impossible to a man!"

"It is not fair Jamie should take the risk," Macey protested.

"Nonsense," Forbes retorted. "He is well able to take care of himself."

"And what if he is discovered and questioned on who helped him to enter Huntly House?" Macey asked.

"They would not learn anything from me," Jamie maintained.

Forbes's face had changed, however, at this prospect, and he said thoughtfully, "d'Aquirre will be there. If *he* were to find you —"

He turned abruptly to Marie. "I cannot allow it," he announced. "I know d'Aquirre and I know his methods. He is skilled in torture and cold-blooded as a fish. If this boy is taken and put to the question by him he would tell everything he knew — he would be glad to tell once d'Aquirre had his way with him! Then your part in the affair would come to light. You, too, would be taken and put to the question. No, Marie, no! I cannot allow it."

A babble of protest broke from both Marie and Jamie. Macey silenced them both with a shout and caught at Forbes's arm as he turned grimly away.

"There is one way to settle it," he said. "Mistress Marie, is there an outer door near the turret that you can leave unlocked?"

"Yes, there is one a few steps away from it," Marie said.

"Then here is what I propose," Macey told Forbes. "Angus Mhor will stay outside Mistress Marie's door tonight. At the first sign of trouble Jamie will raise such a hubbub that Angus cannot fail to hear him, and he will then take her quickly to the door by the turret. You and I will be waiting outside it. We, too, will hear Jamie's cries and will enter by the door she has left unlocked. There will then be three of us to cover Mistress Marie's escape. We will have caddies standing by to escort her safely home and then we three can turn our swords to the rescue of Jamie."

Breathlessly the other two waited to hear what Forbes would say. "How many are expected at the meeting, Marie?" he asked cautiously.

"Six, including Huntly himself," she answered.

"H'm, outnumbered two to one," Forbes commented.

"You forget our young swordsman here," Macey reminded him.

"That is true," Forbes agreed. "Now it is six to four and my sword is worth two of Huntly's own. D'Aquirre is not much of a swordsman either."

"Tod Carmichael is a grand fellow to have by your side in a fight," Jamie ventured. "And the Cleek can crack skulls right handily yet with his golf club for all he is old."

"So I have heard," Forbes chuckled.

"Then all we need now is two stout fellows to escort Mistress Marie home if the need arises," Macey remarked.

"You can trust Cuddy and Daddler — the two that

watched for you at the Bow — for that," Jamie said confidently.

"Let us settle on times then," Macey went on briskly. "Mistress Marie, when does the meeting take place?"

"The half-hour after nine o'clock," Marie told him, "but you will have to leave here in time to get through the Netherbow Port and into the Canongate before the city gates are closed for the night."

"We could all meet at Highland Meg's ale house in the Canongate," Forbes suggested. "She is third cousin to Angus Mhor and will know how to keep silence about our presence there. The stroke of the Canongate church clock can be heard both there and at Huntly House, and so the hour of nine striking could be our signal. We will leave the ale house when we hear it and make quickly for the passageway at the side of Huntly House while Marie ties the rope in position. Agreed?"

There was a chorus of "Agreed!"

Macey glanced at the fading light outside the windows. "We will have to hurry," he pointed out. "The day is fast dying. Jamie, run quickly and fetch the other four caddies to meet us forthwith at Highland Meg's. Waste no time in explanation. They can hear Mistress Marie's plan when we meet."

Quickly Jamie reached for his discarded doublet and cloak and as he scrambled into them Forbes said resignedly to Marie,

"You are a managing hussy, miss. Pray, for your own sake, that it does not come to a battle."

"Nonsense, Papa!" she retorted. "You are spoiling for a fight, all of you — you and M'sieu Macey *and* Jamie!"

"And she is perfectly right!" thought Jamie as he ran

swiftly to fetch the other caddies. It would be a good night's work if he could overhear everything that went on and escape unscathed, but an even better one if an opportunity arose to use his new sword in a real battle!

8. The Spanish Letters

The small dim-lit room in Highland Meg's was crowded with the seven of them gathered there — Macey, Forbes, and Jamie, with Cleek and Tod and the other two caddies, Cuddy and Daddler. Eight o'clock had already boomed out from the Canongate church clock, and as the final hour passed conversation petered out and died into a tense silence of expectation. Glancing round them, Jamie saw each man absorbed in his own thoughts and envied them their apparent calm as he counted off the last moments of waiting.

Nine o'clock struck. Swiftly all seven of them were on their feet and heading for the door. In the darkness of the street they scattered, each one slipping separately through the shadows towards the archway at the side of Huntly House.

Jamie saw it suddenly looming up ahead of him, a wide cave of shadow. He plunged through it and emerged into a paved passageway. The side wall of Huntly House was on his left hand. He glanced up and saw the turret projecting, as Marie had described, at first floor level, and directly below it his hand touched a rope swinging gently against the stone.

"Quickly, Jamie, quickly!" Macey's voice breathed with sudden urgency at his ear. "There are guards patrolling the outside of the house!"

He heard the footsteps of a guard — heavy, steel-shod footsteps, as Macey spoke, and leapt for the rope. "Pull it up after you!" Macey hissed, then he was climbing rapidly hand over hand, muscles straining to the last spark of effort as the beat of the steel feet rang louder on the paving.

The window ledge rose before his face. He transferred his grip to the sill and heaved till he was in position to wriggle through the narrow window opening. Hands groping, he slid blindly down into the interior of the turret. Cold smooth stone met his touch as he reached the floor and with a quick twist and scramble he was on his feet and jerking the rope back into the prayer closet with him.

Cautiously, as it dropped in a coil at his feet, he looked down from the window. The guard whose footsteps he had heard was advancing from the direction of the stables, ponderously marching down the centre of the passageway. There was no sign of Macey or the others but his warning had shown they were alive to the unexpected presence of the guard and so presumably they were well hidden.

He waited for the guard to pass but the man halted beneath the turret window, and just in time Jamie jerked back out of the line of his upward glance. For the space of half a minute he stood with his back pressed against the wall of the prayer closet, his heartbeats sounding loudly in the silence and stifling darkness of the tiny space. A renewed clank of metal on stone broke the stillness suddenly, and on a long, soundless breath of relief he listened to the guard's footsteps receding down the passage.

With his hands held out exploringly, he felt round the confines of the closet. There was room in it only for the prayer-desk to which Marie had tied the rope. The carved screen was, in fact, the door that gave access to the closet from the salon beyond, and kneeling down he peered through the spaces fretted in the woodwork's elaborate design. The room was dark, with only the vague outlines of its furnishings discernible. There was time yet, however, for the conspirators to gather, and pulling the kneeling stool of the *prie-dieu* towards him he squatted down on it to wait their arrival.

A light springing up beyond the screen was his first warning. Cautiously Jamie applied his eye again to a space in the carving and saw a servant-girl, taper in hand, lighting the candles in their wall-sconces. She drew the shutters, flicked her apron over the silver inkstand on the long, polished top of the table running down the centre of the room, and pattered out again.

Voices came from beyond the door. It swung open and a small dark man whom Jamie recognized as the Earl of Huntly came in. Sempill followed him, laughing back over his shoulder at the two men behind him. Crawford and Errol, Jamie placed these other two, and the fair-haired man close on their heels was Hamilton. Lastly came d'Aquirre, walking more slowly than the others, his dress of deepest black in sombre contrast to their brilliant silks and velvets.

He stood at the head of the table, thin lips unsmiling, his very quietness compelling the other five to attention. Chairs scraped as they seated themselves while d'Aquirre placed the black leather folder he carried on the table in front of him. Taking a sheaf of papers from it he tapped them with a long thin forefinger. In a cold, precise voice and with a pronunciation that sounded strange to Jamie's Edinburgh ears, he began,

"Messieurs, let us be brief. These letters written at our last meeting on the twenty-fourth evening of January are now translated into cypher. They await your signature before being sent on their way to His Spanish Majesty."

He turned to Huntly, seated on his right. "My lord of Huntly, will you please to sign your letter first?"

"You are moving too fast, too fast, d'Aquirre,"

Huntly said. "You promised a settlement of the gold and we have seen none of it yet."

"I promised nothing," d'Aquirre said coldly, "except that King Philip would provide the gold to pay for the troops you will raise to meet his own when they land at Leith. That is when our settlement will take place, my lord, and until then the gold will stay safely in my care."

Hubbub broke out around the table at this speech. There were shouts of "*Infamous!*" and "*How can we wage troops with promises?*" Huntly jumped to his feet his face red with rage, and strutting up and down like a fiery little bantam cock he harangued the meeting. Fascinated, Jamie watched from behind the screen, his eyes on Sempill tilted back in his chair and smiling at the ceiling and on d'Aquirre waiting in contemptuous silence for the uproar to subside.

"You may withdraw from the enterprise if you wish, my lord Huntly," he said when order was eventually restored, "but if you do your preparations to date will have been wasted and — I need hardly warn you — you cannot hope to succeed in restoring your country to the Church of Rome without the help of Philip of Spain. I advise you, my lord, to accept our terms."

There was a mutter and silence. "Very well, we agree," Huntly said sulkily. "We have no choice. But there is another matter on which *we* will make the terms, d'Aquirre. If we are to keep our king a prisoner and issue proclamations over his name, the seat of government must also be in our hands. Therefore we must take Edinburgh and Edinburgh Castle or the people will not believe that King James is our leader. But there is one man who could stand between us and this purpose and so we must take him in on our side."

"You are referring to the Earl of Bothwell," Sempill

said suddenly, “and he is of the Protestant faith. Why should *he* join with you?”

“Bothwell hates England and the English queen more than he loves the Reformed Kirk,” Huntly sneered. “He cares not whether it be Spanish troops or any other that despoil her land. And as for us, we have decided not to move without him. We can hold the north unaided, but he is such a power in the Border country that we must have his help to hold the south once Edinburgh is in our hands.”

Sempil glanced up the table to d’Aquirre. “It is sound strategy,” he commented. “It would help to secure the rear of the Spanish forces and lessen the risk of their being cut off on the invasion march to London.”

“Yes, yes,” d’Aquirre said impatiently, “but time is of the essence now, messieurs. Who knows what delay it will cause to bring this new ally in!”

“We have come prepared for that,” Huntly said. “We have been in touch with Bothwell for some time past and he is willing to join us once he knows we are agreed on including him in the plan.”

“So, you have divulged our secrets to this Protestant nobleman, d’Aquirre said menacingly.

“He has kept good faith with our confidence as we have with yours,” Huntly snapped.

D’Aquirre’s thin lips stretched in a mockery of a smile. “There will be no heads left to keep secrets in if the case proves otherwise,” he said.

“Save your threats, d’Aquirre,” Huntly returned. “We have granted your condition over the gold. Now you must grant ours in this matter of strategy.”

The other lords murmured agreement and d’Aquirre asked abruptly, “How long would it take to obtain word from Bothwell?”

"He is in the Border country just now," Huntly said. "We should have to allow two days for a messenger to ride there and two days for him to return."

"Very well, four days," d'Aquirre agreed. "But no longer, you understand! King Philip is impatiently waiting to hear of our arrangements for the landing of his troops and these letters cannot be delayed any further. Now, my lords, your signatures if you please."

He placed a letter in front of Huntly and pushed the inkstand towards him. After a momentary hesitation Huntly dipped the quill in the ink and signed. Quickly d'Aquirre distributed a letter each to the others and the quill was passed around for their signatures. A general buzz of conversation broke out. It was too confused for Jamie to catch more than a word here and there, and withdrawing from the screen he sank back on the stool to collect his thoughts.

The pattern of the spies' activities was clear now. Philip of Spain *was* planning to invade England again, this time with the support of traitor Scottish nobles. The Spanish troops would land at Leith, meet with the rebel Scots and march south on London. Meanwhile, Huntly would take King James prisoner. He would issue proclamations to make it appear that the Scottish king approved the Spaniards' attack on England, and his reward would be in gold and in Philip's help in restoring the power of the Roman Church in Scotland.

The letters now being signed were to be King Philip's signal that all was ready for the attack, and they would probably have been dispatched on the Netherlands ship that night had it not been for the traitor lords' determination to include Bothwell in the plan. He must be that "*one other whose name I have yet to learn*" mentioned in Norton's letter, thought Jamie, and a slow boil of anger began in his blood at the plotters gathered on the other side of the screen.

"Traitors! Filthy traitors!" he mouthed silently. His hand went out to touch the hilt of his sword and froze there as d'Aquirre's voice sounded almost in his ear.

"Madame, the Countess, is well now I trust, my lord?" he was saying in suave tones.

"She is improving," Huntly's voice replied equally close to him, and turning his head Jamie realized that the chinks of light in the screen were gone, blotted out by the bodies of the two men. They must have moved down the room to talk privately, he thought, as Huntly went on,

"She has found a cure for her migraine, I understand. A Mam'selle Marie Forbes has been treating her she tells me, and with success."

"Marie Forbes?" d'Aquirre asked sharply.

"Daughter to John Forbes the fencing master — surely a man of your experience, m'sieur, has heard of John Forbes!"

"Yes, yes, of course," d'Aquirre said lightly. "So his daughter is treating your wife, my lord. That is interesting."

"She has great skill in leechcraft, I believe," Huntly said carelessly, "though she is not much above sixteen years of age. I am told she treats the poor of the city and will never refuse to answer a call for help."

There was a pause in which Jamie held his breath for d'Aquirre's next remark. "A generous and accomplished miss, it would appear," he said at last in a tone that seemed to indicate he had lost interest in the subject. Or had he? He had no reason, after all, to think that either John Forbes or his daughter knew anything about him, Jamie argued to himself.

He peered through the screen again as they moved

away from it, still talking. D'Aquirre was gathering up the signed letters and replacing them in his folder. The others were picking up cloaks and hats preparatory to departure and Sempill was already waiting at the door, plumed hat swinging impatiently in his hand as he waited for d'Aquirre.

Whatever the man in black had thought or suspected about Marie there was evidently no intention of pursuing the subject that night. Both he and Sempill had the air of men eager to depart, Jamie decided, and suddenly inspiration struck him. If he could get down from the prayer closet quickly enough and find Macey and Forbes, they could quietly follow the two men, waylay them and rob them of the Spanish Letters! The evidence essential to support an accusation of Huntly to the king would be in their hands. He would *have* to believe them in the face of such proof and the whole plot would be foiled!

Hurriedly he groped for the coil of rope and crawled with it to the window. His arm was raised to cast it down when a movement below caught his eye. The steel-helmeted outline of the guard took shape. He was standing with his back to the wall of the house across the passage from Huntly House, a position from which he could not fail to see the rope as it came hurtling down.

Switching the rope to his left hand, Jamie drew his sword and stood debating his next move. He could throw the rope down, slide down it one-handed with his sword in the other ready to meet the guard's attack. But long before he reached the ground, he realized, the man would have raised an alarm that would bring his fellow-guards running. An open battle between his own and the Huntly forces would be certain to follow and the spies would certainly not await the outcome of it. They would flee with all speed, and not only would the letters be gone, the rope would be discovered and Mistress Marie put in danger, and the whole success of Macey's mission jeopardized.

Reluctantly he sheathed his sword again and waited at the window in an agony of frustration. Macey and Forbes would not think of following the plotters when they left — not until he, himself, was safely out of Huntly House. Yet he could not escape till the guard was dealt with and the others could not risk doing that until the coast was clear again! It was a vicious circle, he thought desperately, and gritted his teeth at the thought that every passing second was taking the Spanish Letters further and further away.

There was complete silence now round Huntly House. The soft footsteps of the plotters, as they left it, had died completely away, but still the guard stood stolidly beneath the window. He kicked at a stone with his foot. It rattled down the passage and with a yawn and a shrug of boredom he sauntered after it, and passing through the archway turned to glance down the street.

For an instant only Jamie saw the man outlined there in light reflected from a window opposite, then a shadow loomed up behind him. The shadow raised an arm and brought it down in a violent chopping motion on the back of the guard's neck. He sagged soundlessly, his body was caught and held, and the shadowy assailant became the form of Macey running silently up the passageway.

Jamie was half over the sill when Macey's voice hissed up to him. "Loose the rope and cast it down. Jump! We will break your fall!"

Other shadowy forms appeared and grouped beneath the window. Hurriedly Jamie scrambled back into the prayer closet, loosed the rope from the *prie-dieu* and cast it down to them. He poised on the window-sill, held his breath as if for a dive, and jumped.

The group went down under his weight. His head struck violently against the ground, and with the breath knocked from him by the fall he gasped in a tangle of bodies, arms, and legs. In a daze he heard Macey whisper, "Are you hurt, boy?" He gasped an assurance. "Then hurry!" It was Forbes, grasping his other arm and propelling him between himself and Macey towards the archway.

The Cleek rose at their approach from beside the prone body of the guard. As they swung past him and into the street he joined them with the hoarse whisper, "I have cut his purse and bloodied his head with my cleek. It will look like a street robbery now."

Tod's voice came from behind them, "I have the rope safe."

"Then Marie is clear of suspicion, thank God!" Forbes muttered, and Macey responded fervently, "Amen!"

The voices all seemed to Jamie to come from far off. He stumbled along half-carried between Forbes and Macey, only vaguely realising that they were hurrying to reach cover before the alarm was raised with the discovery of the wounded guard.

"Bear up!" Macey encouraged him. "'Tis only a few steps now to Highland Meg's."

The fear of pursuit that the words implied pierced through the fog in Jamie's brain. His steps steadied, allowing the others to increase their pace. Half-running, they arrived in a body at the ale house door. The Highlandwoman was waiting for them. The door swung open without the need to knock and they crowded through it back into the sanctuary of the room they had left earlier that evening.

9. Pursuit of a Spy

"On to the settle with you, Jamie," Macey directed. "Let us see the extent of that injury to your head."

He parted Jamie's hair with careful fingers and examining the blood-encrusted wound decided, "'Twill need bathing before we can tell."

"I will fetch water and a napkin," Tod offered.

He disappeared from the room and Macey said kindly, "I am sorry about the jump, lad, but we did not reckon on the guard round the house. We had to strike down the one at the turret to let you escape but we knew that when his fellows found him insensible they would search for his assailant and find the rope before Mistress Marie could recover it. As it is now, his cut purse and bloodied head will make our attack look like the work of a night-robber. And thanks to that brave leap of yours they will find nothing to cast suspicion on Mistress Marie."

"There is no harm done then, so long as she is safe," Jamie said, and managed a smile in spite of his aching head.

Forbes clapped him on the shoulder with, "Good lad! She will puzzle over the rope's disappearance, of course, but if she is not questioned about it she will have sense enough to know we must have taken it ourselves. But for my part, I shall be glad when Angus Mhor takes her home in the morning and she is safe out of this business."

There was a general murmur of agreement, then Macey said, "Tell us what happened then, Jamie. But take it slowly — that was a nasty fall you took."

Slowly, as Macey had advised, Jamie recounted the

conspirators' talk. Forbes and Macey listened with an astonished anger that showed how clearly they were linking it with the previously known parts of the puzzle. They heard him out in silence, however, until he had finished by telling them how the Spanish Letters had slipped from their grasp. Forbes said immediately then:

"They will have made for Leith, Macey. The road from the Canongate runs direct there and they cannot get back into the city tonight any more than we can."

"'Tis the likeliest place to find them, for the time being at any rate," the Cleek agreed.

"Then we must pin them down there," Macey announced grimly. "Bothwell's inclusion in the plan has given us this four days of grace in which to capture the letters before they leave the country. We *must* succeed in laying hands on them within that time if we are to foil the Spanish king's invasion plans. And that means tracking Sempill and d'Aquirre openly now, with every resource we can muster! Cleek! How many caddies are there in the city?"

"Almost two hundred and fifty, counting boys like Jamie," the Cleek told him.

"I want every one of them in Leith tomorrow morning," Macey commanded. "Send Cuddy and Daddler here back into the city at dawn to muster them. We others will go ahead to Leith, set up headquarters in the Ship Inn and organize the search from there."

Tod's reappearance at that moment brought Macey's attention back to Jamie. He leaned over the back of the settle, watching as the big man gently bathed the hair free from the caked blood on his temple.

"'Tis on the surface only, Mr Macey," Tod said, looking over Jamie's head to him. He folded the wet napkin and laid it like a compress over the wound. "There, boy, you will be in fine fettle by the morning," he said reassuringly. "Stretch out on the settle now and sleep."

"There is not room for us all to stretch out in this small space," Jamie protested, struggling to sit up. "'Tis not fair to favour me above the rest."

Gently Tod pressed him down again, and shrugging off his cloak Macey rolled it into a bundle and placed it under his head. "Rest as you are told," he commanded, "or you will not be fit in the morning."

The fine velvet of the cloak was soft and comforting against his throbbing head, and suddenly Jamie felt too tired to protest any further. Gratefully he stretched out and pillowed his head on it. The room swam round him in a blur of flickering shadows and a murmur of men's voices, and he was asleep.

The Cleek's hand on his shoulder shaking him into wakefulness brought him back to the chill grey light of the following morning. He sat up, with one hand going tenderly to his brow. His face was stiff and sore around the temple but otherwise, as Tod had predicted, he was in fine fettle.

"Cuddy and Daddler are away back into the city for the others," the Cleek told him, "and Tod has gone ahead to Leith to engage a room in the Ship Inn."

"Come and break your fast," Macey called, and Jamie joined him and Forbes at the tray where the Highlandwoman had set out a plate of oaten bread and ale. He ate and drank quickly, gripped by their common desire to be off, then Forbes led the way out of the ale house with the other three following, Jamie walking between the Cleek and Macey.

The fencing master kept ahead of them striding down Leith Wynd. He had the solitary look of a man who knows himself at odds with others, and nodding after him Macey said, "There goes a man who will die rather than yield. I cannot persuade him to back down over Sempill. The most he will agree to is that when he is found we will start even in the race to take him."

"We might slip you word secretly when he is found," the Cleek suggested.

"'Tis no use," Macey said. "He will stick closer by my side than a brother when we reach the Ship Inn."

The smell of Leith began to reach them, a smell of tar and salt and rotting fish. Forbes slackened his pace and turned as they caught up, his face wrinkling with distaste. "Dirty Leith!" he quoted, and Jamie said cheerfully, "The Leith folk say the same about Edinburgh, Master Forbes!"

The fencing master grunted and fell into step with them. The smell grew stronger as they entered the town. Seagulls wheeled and hovered, screaming, overhead. Brewers' drays made the cobbles noisy with their clattering, and down on the quayside by the Ship Inn a pungent smell arose from the cattle-hides being loaded on to a French ship.

"Dirty, noisy, *and* foul-smelling," Macey remarked.

He stood gazing at the Netherlands ship riding out in the roads. She sat high in the water, canvas furled and cordage neat. Her decks, as usual, were deserted, and Forbes remarked, "She will not sail this tide at any rate."

As they turned to the inn the Cleek beckoned the group of caddies on the quayside to follow them. Tod met them at the door.

"There is a room at the top of the stairs ready for you, Mr Macey," he said.

"Good man, Tod," Macey replied. "Hold the door down here and let twelve men at a time upstairs for instructions."

"The first dozen of you lads upstairs, the rest back on watch at the quayside," Tod called.

"There is no one will get past Tod that should not," Jamie remarked, grinning to Macey as they climbed upstairs.

"There is no one will get past anyone, anywhere, this day." Macey replied grimly.

He seated himself behind a table in the room. Forbes went to stand by the window overlooking the quay. Jamie retired discreetly into the background, and the Cleek rapped with his golf club on the table to call the caddies to attention.

"The search is the same, men," Macey told them, "except that Leith is now the place where they are almost certain to be found and you will enquire openly for them. Speak freely to the citizens. Describe Sempill and d'Aquirre and warn those you speak to that they are Spanish spies who seek the life of the king. Search inwards from the outer perimeter of the town so that there is nowhere for them to flee once they are flushed from cover. The Cleek will allot each of you the section you must search."

The Cleek took over from this point, splitting the group into pairs and allotting each an area of search. "Keep together in your pairs," he instructed, "one to run back here like the wind with any news uncovered and the other to stand watch while he does so."

He lifted his cleek menacingly and growled, "I will split the head of any man that misuses my instructions. You understand?"

"They understand very well — we all do!" Jamie said silently to himself as he watched them troop off. And suddenly it occurred to him to wonder how it was that the old man kept his hold over such a band of rough, fearless fellows as the caddies. As if answering his unspoken thought, Macey said quietly to him:

"Such authority is born in a man, not made. And he has it in rare measure."

There was a lull before the next group of caddies arrived, but they were the first of those that Cuddy and Daddler had gathered from Edinburgh and after that the others crowded in thick and fast. Jamie and Forbes were pressed into service to repeat Macey's original instructions while the Cleek, unflustered by the constant stream of men past him, calmly went on with his recital of street-names for each pair of searchers.

"There is a net now that not even a minnow could slip through," he remarked with a satisfied air when the last pair had vanished through the door.

"And all we can do now is to wait till it is drawn," Macey added.

He leaned forward, rubbing one hand over his haggard face. Jamie glanced out of the window, noting how high the tide had crept up against the quayside since they arrived. It must be noon already, he thought, wondering at how the morning had vanished under the rush of organising the search.

The appearance of serving-women with soup and bread for their party, confirmed his thought. "I will take some to Tod," he offered, and with the two bowls and the bread balanced in his hands went downstairs. They ate ravenously, dipping the hunks of bread in the soup, but when the bowls were cleared and there was nothing to do but wait Jamie began to find the slow passage of time irksome.

Discontentedly scanning the traffic of the street he said, "I would rather be with the others searching than sitting here, would you not, Tod?"

"Your turn will come," Tod said wisely. "The real action is yet to be, Jamie."

They sat on, making way for the occasional caddie returning to retail some report he had heard, hoping each time that it would lead to the promised action, but no word came down from the room upstairs. It was Cuddy, at last, who proved to be the bearer of real news.

He came running up, eyes starting out from a face tense with excitement. Tod and Jamie leapt up and Tod grabbed at Cuddy's arm. "Tell us!" he commanded.

"The Anchor Inn — only two streets away!" Cuddy gasped. "Sempill and the captain of the Netherlands ship!"

Breaking free of Tod's hand he dashed upstairs, Jamie and Tod pounding after him. Macey, Forbes, and the Cleek had risen at the sound of their feet on the stairs. They were facing the door in a tense group as the other three burst into the room. Forbes broke away from it and strode over to Cuddy, grasping him by the front of the doublet.

"Sempill — where is he?" he rasped.

Cuddy opened his mouth to gasp the news again but Macey leapt forward and clapped his hand over his face.

"Cleek!" he shouted. "Call up every caddie in earshot to surround any place that Cuddy names. Capture Sempill alive if he breaks free of it!"

The Cleek made a hobbling rush for the window and leaned out whistling shrilly on his fingers. Macey released his hold on Cuddy and stepped back. "We bargained to start even, Forbes," he said. "Now Cuddy can talk."

"Sempill and the Spanish captain," Cuddy gasped. "They are at the Anchor Inn!"

A split second took Macey and Forbes to the door with Forbes shouting, *"He's mine now, mine, Macey!"*

and Jamie's voice rising above it in a shriek of, "*I know the place, Mr Macey. Follow me!*" as he hurtled down the stairs ahead of them both.

Neck and neck they raced up the first twenty yards of the street then Macey, the longest-legged of the three, shook Forbes off and began to outpace Jamie.

"Turn right, left, and right again," Jamie gasped as he drew ahead. "You will see the sign of the Anchor."

Still running, he looked back over his shoulder and saw Forbes turning up an alley they had just passed. "There must be a short cut that way," he thought in dismay and turned with a warning shout to Macey pounding ahead of him. Macey glanced back. It was a fatal move. A carter walking backwards as pulled at the rein of the mule in his charge cannoned into him. Macey's feet slid from under him. The mule kicked out. Its hoof caught the side of Macey's head and sent him sprawling on his back on the cobbles.

Within seconds he and the carter were the centre of a shouting, pushing mob. Jamie thrust through it, angrily elbowed the carter away from Macey, and kneeling down took his head on his knee. Macey was conscious, but dazed, and seeing no help for it Jamie slapped briskly at both sides of his face.

"Rouse up! Rouse up, Mr Macey!" he commanded urgently. "Forbes is ahead of us!"

Macey groaned and shook his head. He pushed Jamie's hands away and scrambled to his feet. "Make way, make way, he is not hurt!" Jamie shouted, pushing back at the curious mob. They fell back, and grasping Macey firmly by the arm Jamie pulled him clear.

He was steady on his feet now. They walked the first few steps then their pace quickened to a trot. Jamie dropped his hold on Macey's arm and they ran on steadily together.

"How much of a start has Forbes?" Macey panted.

"A few minutes only," Jamie reassured him, "and look, there is the Anchor Inn."

The inn sign swung before them a few yards away. The door stood wide open. They plunged in and found themselves in a room that opened directly off the street. There was no need to enquire for either Forbes or Sempill. Facing them at the other side of the room was a stairway to an upper floor, and at the foot of it a knot of men stood gazing upwards, their faces astonished and alarmed.

They burst through the men scattering them on either side and pounded up the stairs. A sharp turn right at the head of the stairs led on to a short passage. A door stood slightly open at the end of this and from the room beyond came shouts and the clash of steel. Simultaneously, they unsheathed their swords.

"Stand guard inside this door! Let no one pass you," Macey snapped.

He thrust at the door with his foot. It flew wide open and they saw Forbes at the far side of the room. He was fighting with his back to the wall, both Sempill and the Spanish captain pressing hard to beat down his guard.

A shout from Macey turned the Spaniard towards him and in a flying leap towards one another they were engaged. Forbes pressed outwards from the wall in single combat now with Sempill. Jamie pulled the door shut behind him and with his back to it and sword held ready awaited the outcome of the two battles.

Macey and the Spaniard were the nearer of the two pairs. Macey was the taller of these two and the impossibility of manoeuvring in the confined space made his long reach an advantage. But the Spaniard fought well.

He yielded no ground and for the first few minutes the barrier of blades between them remained unbreakable. Yet he was tiring under the speed of Macey's attack, Jamie noted. He would *have* to yield that one step!

As if willed to do so by the strength of his thought, the Spaniard backed a step and Macey's long reach flickered through his guard. He leapt back, recovered, and lunged again, but Macey was pressing home his advantage now, driving him backwards step by step to the window in the side wall. The Spaniard's heels came hard up against the wooden skirt of the window seat. In the second that his balance was lost Macey struck and the sword went flying from his opponent's hand.

"Your prisoner, Jamie!" he shouted, and in a lightning swoop Jamie was across the room, his sword-point at the Spaniard's chest pushing him down on to the window seat and pinning him there. Macey whirled away and circled sword in hand round the battle between Forbes and Sempill.

"Surrender, Sempill!" he shouted. "Forbes will kill you but you have a chance for life if you surrender to me!"

"You are wrong!" Sempill shouted. "*I* will kill Forbes!"

He laughed exultantly, teeth gleaming in the golden-red of his beard. "*A bonny fighter*," Lucky had called him, Jamie thought, and Forbes had said he was almost as good a swordsman as himself. It was hard to judge what would be the outcome of their meeting!

Sempill's style had a recklessness and bravado about it that made it seem impossible for anyone to stand against him — anyone except Forbes! The fencing master was fighting with ferocious skill, his coolness showing his master of the craft. Yet still, as Macey's hesitation showed he realized clearly, they were too evenly matched for him to interfere on either side.

Both men were out to kill, and in the second that Macey intervened to upset the balance of their skill one of them was certain to be run through by the other's sword. The only chance he had of effecting a capture, Jamie calculated, was that one should disarm the other. If Macey was quick enough then in leaping in to parry the death-stroke from the remaining blade, he would be able to regain control of the situation.

Meanwhile there was no slackening in the speed of their encounter and neither seemed to have any advantage over the other. They circled, closed and broke again with rapid skill and tireless energy, until even the Spanish captain forgot his resentment at the role of prisoner and watched with the same breathless interest as Jamie.

Suddenly a gasping cry from Sempill sounded above the clash of blades. He closed body to body with Forbes. Their left hands gripped, their swords crossed almost at the hilt locked in a pressure that forced the blades high in the air.

It was a desperately defensive move on Sempill's part. Forbes cleared himself of it with a savage thrust of his right forearm, and as Sempill leapt back from the stroke that followed, Jamie saw the reason for his tactics. He was wounded in the upper part of the sword-arm, and the stain of blood spreading rapidly over the sleeve of his doublet showed that Forbes's blade had penetrated deeply.

Once again, Sempill lunged. The timing was a fraction out and his weakened grip robbed the stroke of the power it needed. Forbes's blade met the lunge in a powerful parrying stroke that sent Sempill's weapon flying across the room. Jamie had one glimpse of his astonished and horrified face, then Forbes struck.

In the flicker of time it took for his sword to drive straight at Sempill's heart, a number of things happened simultaneously. Macey leapt between him and Sempill, his left hand swinging in a back-handed blow that sent Sempill spinning from the line of danger, the sword in his right hand flashing out to strike up Forbes's blade. And from the doorway the voice of d'Aquirre came in a shout of, "*Lieutenant Forbes!*"

10. Deadlock

Instinctively Jamie wheeled round — as did Macey and Forbes, to the direction of d'Aquirre's voice and in the unguarded second of his surprise was sent sprawling over the window seat by a blow from the Spaniard's fist.

Through the ringing in his ears he was aware of d'Aquirre saying, "I see that the years since Liège have not taught you wisdom, Lieutenant Forbes," and Forbes snarling in reply:

"You always rated your own cunning too high, d'Aquirre, but I will live to see both you and Sempill wiped from the face of the earth."

He looked up, shaking the muzziness from his head. D'Aquirre was still standing in the doorway and the Spanish captain had reached the protection of the group of armed men crowding behind him in the passage.

"You have had your opportunity with Sempill," d'Aquirre was saying, "and now, as you can see, you are outnumbered."

He made as if to advance into the room but Forbes and Macey leapt forward, shoulder to shoulder, and Forbes roared:

"You will be the first to die, d'Aquirre!"

It was a bold, a desperate challenge, but it would not save them, Jamie thought grimly. There was no one who could do that now — except the Cleek. Huddled back on the window seat he scanned the street below intently as d'Aquirre replied:

"I do not practise foolish gallantry as you do. I have —"

"I have had enough of your talk! Draw your blade, man!" Forbes interrupted.

D'Aquirre made some reply to this but Jamie never heard it for just at that moment he caught the sound of the Cleek's long, shrill whistle and saw the end of the street where the inn stood become suddenly solid with a mass of advancing men.

Scrambling to his feet he turned to d'Aquirre yelling, "Hold your hand, d'Aquirre! "Tis you who are outnumbered now!"

Suspicion and rage replaced the triumph in d'Aquirre's face at the shout. "What nonsense is this?" he demanded.

"No nonsense — look there!" A blow of Jamie's fist sent the casement windows bursting wide open and he flourished an arm in the direction of the street. "There are at least a hundred of stout fellows advancing to our aid!"

A shout of triumph broke from Macey. Springing to the window he glanced swiftly out then turned back to d'Aquirre, still held at bay by Forbes's sword.

"The boy is right," he announced crisply. "We have reinforcements advancing rapidly to surround the inn. You are trapped!"

"*Tod! Cleek!*" Jamie yelled. He leaned from the window, brandishing his sword. The shout and the silver signal of the steel flashing in the sun brought the eyes of the advancing caddies to the window. An answering roar from many voices surged up to them and Forbes jeered:

"You have over-reached yourself this time, d'Aquirre. You will not leave this room alive!"

D'Aquirre smiled his thin-lipped, mirthless smile. "That will indeed be a pity," he remarked coldly, "since the stroke that kills me will undoubtedly kill your daughter also!"

"*My daughter?*" A look of stupefied horror spread over Forbes's face as he whispered the words. Jamie and Macey also stared at d'Aquirre in horrified disbelief, and returning their look with one of malicious triumph he said:

"She is my prisoner. If I die, she dies also!"

With a roar of almost animal anguish Forbes sprang at him, but anticipating the move, Macey leapt between them hurling the fencing master back with all his strength and yelling, "He means it, you fool! For pity's sake Forbes — do you *want* her to die!"

Horrified, Jamie watched as they crashed to the ground with Macey's hands closed round Forbes's throat and choking off his cries. Bending over the fencing master's contorted face he said distinctly, "If Marie's life is at stake we must talk terms. Do you understand?"

Forbes gave a groan of assent. Macey released his grip and as Forbes staggered to his feet he rushed over to the window, pushing Jamie aside.

"Hold your men back, Cleek!" he shouted. "Hold them back! Do not attack presently — do *not* attack presently!"

As his voice died away they were startled to hear Sempill say suddenly, "This is none of my doing, Forbes. I do not war with women, as you well know."

Unnoticed by them all he had regained his feet at some time in the past few minutes and now, ignoring Forbes's spluttered reply, he walked over to d'Aquirre.

"Is this true?" he demanded.

"As true as the fact that these are in my possession," d'Aquirre said calmly.

He felt inside his cloak and withdrew his hand holding a bone-handled dirk carved with an antlered stag's head. "We took this off your servant," he said. "I take it you recognize the weapon?"

"Angus Mhor's dirk!" Forbes whispered. His hand closed round it convulsively and he cried, "It is still not proof! Angus could be wounded to death and still guard my daughter!"

"As to whether he lives or not I could not say," d'Aquirre remarked, "though it took a mightily strong force to bear him down. However, perhaps this will convince you."

He held out between thumb and forefinger a small ring set with amethyst and pearl. Forbes took it and turned it over in his hand. "I am convinced," he said at length. "It was my wife's and Marie has worn it since she died. She would never willingly let it out of her sight."

He looked up at d'Aquirre with hatred blazing in his face. "You can have your life," he snarled, "but only under guarantee of my daughter's safe return. And if you have harmed her —"

"Wait!" d'Aquirre broke into his threat. "I have other terms to make, Forbes — terms that concern the Englishman, Macey."

"I guessed as much," Macey said calmly. "Name them, d'Aquirre."

"First you must agree that neither side attacks the other till I have been heard," d'Aquirre bargained.

"The men below will not move till I tell them — you heard my instructions," Macey returned.

With a shrug of acceptance d'Aquirre closed the door of the room and leant against it. "Well, d'Aquirre," Macey challenged, "Why should the capture of Marie Forbes concern me?"

"Ask the boy," d'Aquirre said maliciously. "It was through him it came about."

"You lie!" Jamie exploded. "How could I have anything to do with such a deed!"

"Be quiet, Jamie," Macey snapped. "Let him speak."

"Cast your mind back to the night you followed me from the house in the Upper Bow," d'Aquirre said to Jamie. "You were not aware, were you, that Sempill's serving-man, Pringle, tracked you that night as you tracked me?"

"No — I — I —" Jamie stammered, and falling back a step he glanced appealingly at Forbes and Macey.

"Stop playing cat and mouse, d'Aquirre," Forbes burst out. "Tell me about my daughter!"

"Very well," d'Aquirre said smoothly. "Pringle's observations that night warned me that Sempill and myself had been spied on. I knew that your concern with Sempill was a personal one. I guessed that Macey's interest in my affairs was political, and I decided to use the one to combat the other."

"Do you mean to tell us that you have been seeking to abduct the girl ever since?" Macey said incredulously.

"I am not a novice in espionage, m'sieur," d'Aquirre replied coldly. "I know the value of holding a move in reserve. Forbes's house has been watched since then, but I saw no reason to move till it was reported to me this morning that you had all left it last night and that only the girl and her servant had returned.

"I was abroad myself on business last night, and with the possibility in mind that your absence from home might have been concerned with a further attempt at meddling in my affairs, I judged the time ripe to take the girl hostage for your future good behaviour. The man-servant provided difficulties, as I have said, but there were a sufficient number of men to over-power him. For the rest, my presence here now is simply the result of a fortunate guess that your continued absence from home meant that you were in pursuit of Sempill."

"You could not have carried Marie from her home in broad daylight," Forbes said hotly. "She is known and loved in Edinburgh — one scream would have brought hundreds to her aid!"

"Very true," d'Aquirre replied blandly. "That is why Pringle had instructions to remove her in a closed litter with a knife at her throat."

Forbes groaned and leaned against the wall with his face in his hands and d'Aquirre pressed viciously on, "There is no one but myself knows where she is now. There is no one to hear her cries for help, no one to bring her food but me, and if I do not return to the place where she is hidden she will die a slow death from starvation!"

"Enough, d'Aquirre!" Sempill broke in. "Name your terms to them."

"Ah yes, the terms," d'Aquirre echoed triumphantly. He looked consideringly from Forbes to Macey. "This is now the seventh day of February," he remarked, "and I expect my business to be brought to a successful conclusion by the eleventh day of the month. The girl will be of no further use to me as a hostage after that date and I will undertake to return her unharmed to you provided that you, Forbes, and you, Macey, consent to return to Forbes's house and undertake not to stir from there till she is released.

"The boy here is not to go near the house in that time, and a guard will be mounted over it night and day to see that the conditions are kept. One suspicious move from any of you and she dies. Do you agree?"

"I have no choice," Forbes groaned.

"And you, M'sieur Macey?"

"I —" Macey began, and hesitated.

"Agree, agree!" Forbes burst out. "Does Marie's life mean nothing to you!"

"It means more than you know," Macey said roughly, "but I have my sworn duty to perform."

He turned away from them and walked over to the window, presenting a rigid back to the room. "We could force the knowledge of her whereabouts from this vile creature," he rasped.

"And if we failed?" Forbes asked bitterly, and answered himself, "She would starve to death!"

Macey bowed his head. In a low voice he said, "Very well. I agree."

D'Aquirre gave a long sigh of satisfaction. "There is nothing more to discuss then," he said, "except that you will give us an hour's start to leave this place — but do not dare to let anyone follow us this time. That would be interpreted as a 'suspicious move' on your part!"

With a baleful glare and a shrug that admitted defeat, Macey leaned out to call the instruction down to the Cleek. D'Aquirre turned to the door, and as Sempill followed him he commented:

"So once again, Colonel Sempill, you are fortunate to escape with your life."

"I expected nothing less in the way of luck," Sempill told him airily. "I am a lucky man — as Forbes knows!"

And with a wave of his hat and a mocking smile to Forbes he followed d'Aquirre through the door.

For a long moment after the door had closed behind them, no one spoke. Quietly Jamie sheathed his sword and waited for Macey to say something but he remained staring out of the window, tight-lipped and pale.

"We have an hour, Mr Macey," Jamie ventured at last. "We should be thinking what to do, surely?"

"Yes." Macey shook himself abruptly out of his brown study. "Yes, we must think." Leaning out of the window he shouted, "Cleek! Hey there, Cleek! Hither to me."

In silence again they waited the old man's stumping steps on the stairs. When he came into the room eventually he was scowling, and sweeping them all sternly with his look he said sourly:

"This is pretty management indeed! We had them penned here like a pair of frightened chickens, then you open the door and let them fly the coop!"

"Hold your noise, you old maggot," Forbes snarled. "Would we have let them go without good reason?"

"d'Aquirre has taken Marie Forbes prisoner and hidden her in some secret place," Macey explained hastily. "He has bargained to release her if we two stay in Forbes's house and make no search for her till four days are past. Jamie is not to come near us in that time and if we do not keep the bargain, she dies."

"Four days!" exclaimed the Cleek. "But the letters—?"

"Will be dispatched by then," Macey finished for him.

"Does d'Aquirre know he was spied on last night, then?" the Cleek demanded of Jamie.

"I would never have been allowed to leave the prayer closet alive if he had known I was there," Jamie pointed out.

"In other words," Macey took up the argument, "we are still one move ahead of him. He knows we spied on Sempill's delivery of the gold, but everything after that is guesswork on his part. The important fact is that *he does not suspect we know about the Spanish Letters!* He cannot therefore suspect that we know the reason for the date he has set for Marie's release, and so there is still a chance of intercepting Sempill before he leaves with the letters."

"True, true," the Cleek agreed cautiously, "but it

will be a very slim chance, Mr Macey. There are a great many 'ifs' and 'buts' in the situation."

"Dear heaven, do you think I do not know that!" Macey exclaimed. "There is no telling the route Sempill will take with the letters. He could sail on the Netherlands ship out there, he could ride out by any of the city gates and go overland to take ship for Spain from the south. The girl might be released within minutes of his leaving — within hours — a day, two days even! So there is no telling either how much of a start he will have over me. He could leave Edinburgh with banners flying and trumpets blowing, and so long as the girl was not safely home there would be nothing I could do to stop him. Nothing!"

An uneasy pause followed this outburst. Jamie gazed out in the silence towards the trim bulk of the Netherlands ship riding gently at her anchor and eventually he asked:

"Why should he go overland to the south if the ship is there waiting for him? Surely it would be easier to sail from Leith?"

"I can think of several reasons," Macey replied gloomily, "not the least of them being that the ship's continued presence there is merely a blind for d'Aquirre's intentions. He must be aware we have guessed it was the method of transport for the gold, and knowing that will choose a less obvious method of dispatching the letters."

"Then all we can do," the Cleek shrugged, "is to keep watching for Sempill leaving the city in the hope you might be able to stop him in time."

"There is nothing else for it," Macey agreed wearily. "But keep a watch on Huntly House also for the arrival of Bothwell's messenger. Sempill will not be long in leaving after he arrives."

The Cleek nodded assent and turned to go, but Forbes stopped him with outstretched hand. "You will do nothing to endanger my daughter," he warned.

The old man looked compassionately at the fencing master's haggard face, "You have my promise on that, on behalf of all the caddies," he re-assured. "Tell your serving-girl to look out for me morning and evening when she goes to the well. 'Twill be a way of keeping in touch if we hear any word of her."

With a sharp, "Come, Jamie!" he left the room. Reluctantly Jamie stepped after him, but at the doorway he hesitated. This *could* not be the end, he thought suddenly. Surely, surely Macey would not accept defeat like this — a defeat that meant invasion and war with Spain for both their countries!

Swinging round on his heel he looked from Forbes to Macey. "There must be something we can do," he said desperately. "Surely there must be *something!*"

"We can do nothing," Forbes said harshly, "except possess our souls in patience till my daughter's safe return."

Macey did not reply at all. His set features gave no clue to his thoughts, and after a moment Jamie turned hopelessly away. Forbes was right, he thought bitterly, there *was* nothing they could do but wait. D'Aquirre had chosen his weapon with devilish skill, for though Macey would face any danger to himself to recover the letters, the death of Marie Forbes was something that none of them could face.

Even so, he found it hard to accept that the position was utterly hopeless, and it was with a sense of burning frustration at the four days' inactivity ahead of them that he eventually followed the Cleek from the inn.

11. Exploration at Night

It was on the afternoon of the fourth day after that frustrating parting at the Anchor Inn that Bothwell's messenger arrived at Huntly House, but Jamie was not aware of it till he returned to the Cleek's cellar in the Potterrow that evening. He had news of his own to report, however, for he had been with those on watch at the gate called the West Port and just before it closed for the night the Earl of Huntly had ridden through it and left the city with a small band of followers.

"— heading north," he told the Cleek.

"Aye, that fits with what we have learned ourselves," the old man said gloomily. "Bothwell's messenger arrived this afternoon, and when Tod spoke with the grooms in the Huntly House stables they told him the Earl was expected to leave soon for Perth."

"Perth?" Jamie looked at him questioningly. "But surely the Huntly stronghold is in Aberdeen?"

"You are forgetting Errol and Crawford are in the plot," the Cleek reminded him. "Perth would be the natural rallying-point for the troops of these three if they meant to launch an attack soon."

"And 'twould be sound strategy to have such a central base for the campaign," Lucky pronounced with the authority of the old campaigner. Tod and Cleek murmured their agreement with this, and with the thought of it casting a gloom over them all their conversation withered and died into silence.

Tod and Lucky settled to sleep eventually while the Cleek continued to sit propped against the wall, brooding like some ancient idol in the pale glow of the lamp in the corner. It became very still in the cellar, so still that even the lamp's wick floated motionless in its boat of oil, but despite the peace that had descended Jamie found it impossible to sleep.

Lying flat on his back on his thin mattress of straw he fixed his eyes on the steady cone of lamplight and let his mind wander gloomily back over the days since he had parted from Forbes and Macey. Nothing had changed for the better since then, he thought despairingly. The watch on the city gates had still revealed no glimpse of either Sempill or d'Aquirre, nor had any of the caddies' spying and questioning brought forth any hint or rumour of Marie's whereabouts.

And so here they were on the eleventh day of the month, still no nearer to capturing the Spanish Letters, and soon — very soon now that Bothwell's messenger had arrived, Sempill would leave the city with them. Yet so long as Marie was in d'Aquirre's hands they were powerless to stop him. They were beaten.

Restlessly, despairing of sleep as the sound of their defeat echoed in his mind, he turned and gazed resentfully at the peaceful forms of Tod and Lucky. The crippled man lay huddled up, an ungainly figure even in sleep, but Tod was stretched full-length on his back, hands crossed on his chest, his massive figure a study in silent repose. The rock-like dignity of his motionless form made Jamie think of the stone figures of the Crusaders on the tombs in Saint Giles's Church. With a superstitious shudder he turned his head away from the stillness that was suddenly too like the stillness of death, and came face to face with the unblinking, lizard-like stare of the Cleek's ancient eyes.

"You should be asleep," the old man said mildly. "What's on your mind?"

Jamie glowered at him. "I am thinking that

Bothwell's messenger arrived today," he said sourly. "I am thinking that it is four days since d'Aquirre hobbled us all to his will and not a cheering piece of news in all that time. How *can* I sleep with matters at such a pass!"

"Ach, you are too easily put down," the Cleek chided him. "It was cheering news to hear that Angus Mhor would live, was it not?"

In spite of himself Jamie's lips twitched in a smile at the remembrance of Nan's report on the Highlander. "*He has lost enough blood to bath a baby in,*" she had told the Cleek, "*but he will be fine now that Master Forbes has patched all the leaks in his skin.*"

"That is more like you now, Jamie," the Cleek approved his smile. "Impatience will not help any of us — as poor Macey is finding out to his cost!"

"Macey?" Jamie sat up eagerly with the question. "Why, what has he done, Cleek?"

"Nothing as yet," the old man sighed, "but I fear me he will do something rash before the time is up. Nan tells me that he and Forbes are at one another's throats all the time now, Macey raging about and swearing he is certain that d'Aquirre has some plan to outwit them over the girl, and Forbes vowing that Macey will leave the house to look for her only over his dead body. And Angus Mhor, now that his strength is coming back to him, is like a caged lion for rage. Nan says it is like living in a house of mad men!"

"Cleek, there is something that puzzles me." Jamie rolled over on to his stomach and looked up intently at the old man. "We started to search for Sempill and d'Aquirre on the first day of February, the day after Macey arrived in Edinburgh, and we have kept a strict watch on the city gates since then. Yet not once has either of them been seen entering or leaving the city.

But we know that they *were* in the city on the night they met at Paterson's house and we know that d'Aquirre at least has been in the city since — on the day he captured Marie Forbes. How is it done? How can they manage to evade our watch?"

"There are ways and means for those that know the secrets of Edinburgh well enough," the Cleek said thoughtfully. "Why, I can remember thirty years back when the king's grandmother, the French woman, Marie de Guise, was Queen of Scotland. There was civil war in the country at one time under her rule and the city was in a state of siege against the French soldiers she called to her aid. Yet still the envoys of the French army were able to pass secretly back and forth from Leith to Edinburgh to talk with her."

"Marie de Guise — the one the de Guise palace was built for?" Jamie asked.

The Cleek nodded. "Aye, the same. It used to be said that there was a secret tunnel under the palace that led down under the gardens and came out on the banks of the Nor Loch and —"

"But that was where the Catholic lords first met!" Jamie interrupted. "At the de Guise palace!"

The Cleek stared at him. "What are you thinking?" he asked slowly. "That d'Aquirre has been using the secret entrance to the palace? That he is hiding there now? That —"

"Wait!" Jamie gestured him to silence. "Wait, there is something I must try to recall."

Leaning forward with his eyes tightly closed he sent his mind roving back into the maze through which he had tracked d'Aquirre on the night that Sempill delivered the gold. The familiar pattern of the narrow alleys spread out in front of his inner vision like a map unfolding, and suddenly memory clicked into place.

That last passage blind to both right and left and with a lower exit opening on to the banks of the loch — the passage in which he had finally lost d'Aquirre! It could only be yards from the place where he and Macey had found Norton's body — only yards away from the bank that marked the foot of the palace gardens!

He sat up with an abrupt, "I have it! It was almost at the foot of the palace gardens I lost d'Aquirre's trail the night I followed him."

"So?" the Cleek probed cautiously.

"So 'tis most likely the way he enters and leaves the city undetected, the most likely place for him to be hidden now — *the place he is almost certain to be holding Mistress Marie captive!*"

Scrambling to his feet on the words, Jamie made a break for the cellar door. And was brought crashing down again as the old man hooked him neatly round the ankle with his cleek.

"You ... you ...!" Spluttering with rage he tried to heave himself to his hands and knees, but the cleek was hooked round his neck now, the iron tip of it bearing painfully down on the big artery under his ear.

"You will hurt yourself if you struggle," the old man was saying mildly. "Lie quiet and listen to me."

Reluctantly Jamie yielded to the cleek's pressure and rolled over, glaring resentfully up at the old man.

"Calm yourself, boy," he was reproved. "Now what were you about to do, eh? Rush out and tell Macey and the girl's father where you *think* she is? But what about the guard on the house — and what happens if you are caught breaking the bargain that you would not go near it?"

"But Macey is afraid d'Aquirre will not keep the bargain himself," Jamie protested. "You told me so only minutes ago."

"Macey is in love with the girl," the Cleek growled. "He has no judgment left where she is concerned. But I have, Jamie, and no rash action of yours is going to endanger her at the last moment. Forbes has my promise on that."

"But —" Jamie protested again, and shrank back under a menacing flourish of the cleek.

"Enough!" The sweet reason had gone from the old man's tone now and his voice was harshly threatening. "I have listened to you enough, Jamie. Tomorrow is the date set for the girl's release, and it will be time enough then to go looking for her at the de Guise palace if d'Aquirre does not keep his part of the bargain. But until then we stick to the letter of it."

Jamie's eyes dropped under his implacable gaze and slowly he sank back on to the rough sacking of his pillow. The Cleek eased himself forward and snuffed out the flame of the lamp. His mattress rustled as he settled back on it and his voice came warningly through the darkness.

"No tricks now, Jamie, or you will have a stronger taste of the cleek than you have ever had!"

Jamie made no reply. A resolution had begun to form in his mind, a resolution that hardened as his fingers slid down to touch the sheathed weapon by his side. When the Cleek slept — as sleep he surely must some time tonight — he would creep from the cellar. But he would not break his bargain by going to Forbes's house. Instead, he would go direct to the place on the banks of the Nor Loch where the entrance to the tunnel into the de Guise palace might be.

After that — well, there was no telling. If he found his way into the palace and discovered Mistress Marie there it might just be possible to rescue her single-handed. It would all depend on how she was guarded.

But if he *did* manage to rescue her, it would set Macey free to try and capture Sempill before he left with the Spanish Letters. It was only a few hours after all since Bothwell's messenger had arrived, and unless Sempill had been standing by to leave on the instant he must still be in hiding somewhere in Leith or Edinburgh. They had caught him once before by raising the hue and cry — they could do so again!

He closed his eyes, schooling himself to wait. The Cleek's breathing became regular, the quick, shallow breaths of an old man asleep. But the Cleek was an old fox, Jamie thought grimly. He might well be feigning sleep. Tensely he waited for the sound of the little bubbling snores that would tell him the old man's sleep was genuine, then inch by inch he eased himself up till he was in a kneeling position. Now was the time for the old man, if he *was* foxing, to sit up suddenly and call out to him!

Bracing himself for the shock of a sudden sound or movement, he knelt motionless, but there was no shout, no move to stop him, and cautiously he crept towards the cellar door. Silently he eased it open just sufficiently to let him slip through, and as silently closed it again behind him.

On tiptoe he stepped off down the street, breaking into a run when he was safely clear of the cellar door. There was no moon to guide him. The city was dark, deserted, dead. The time, he judged, was around two hours after midnight — the time when everyone, prisoner and jailor alike, would be in their deepest sleep.

Running silently, easily, he gained the High Street and passed swiftly through the huddle of the Lawnmarket booths. A narrow opening between the tall houses on the north side of the street swallowed him up and he was once more back in the winding, stinking maze of alleys through which he had tracked d'Aquirre.

This time, however, there were only the minimum deviations necessary to bring him out to the point he sought, and within minutes he saw the opening ahead of him. His skin prickling with remembered fear, he turned into it and ran swiftly towards the further end. The marsh-mud sucked at his feet and he was out again on the bank of the Nor Loch.

It was to the left of this place, he remembered, that he and Macey had stopped at the foot of the palace gardens. Turning left, he plodded off through the squelching mass of mud and reeds. A flight of water-fowl burst cackling from under his feet, and, heart pounding with instinctive terror at the lunatic burst of sound in the darkness, he threw himself sideways. His shoulder struck against a solid mass. Breathless, he regained his balance, and stepping back from the obstruction recognized the wall of banked turf that marked the end of the de Guise palace gardens.

The first flush of triumph at the discovery died quickly as he faced up to the problem of finding the entrance to the tunnel. He could see nothing except that the wall was a dark mass in the surrounding darkness, but the ground, he calculated, would have a hollow ring if the tunnel led beneath it. He stamped tentatively several times. The soggy ground provided no resistance for his feet, and desisting from this effort, he dropped to hands and knees and began to explore with his hands for traces of a trapdoor or other possible entrance.

Nothing but mud, water, and reeds met his probing fingers along the entire length of the ground in front of the wall, and with frustration welling up inside him he rose slowly to his feet again. Mud-covered and dripping, he turned back to the wall. It was all that was left now as a possible concealment for the tunnel entrance, and hopeless as this prospect seemed to be he could not ignore it.

Step by step he moved along the wall and exploring the surface with his hands found it to be an earth bank sloping slightly inwards off the vertical as it rose. It was smoothly faced with thick, close-growing turf, but no projection or hold of any kind me this fingers here either. The entrance, if it was here, was well hidden, but with a stubborn refusal to acknowledge defeat of this last hope Jamie drew his sword and inserted the blade carefully at chest height into the turf of the wall.

The blade slid easily home through the earth and was buried to the hilt. Withdrawing it, he repeated the experiment a few inches further along the wall. Again the blade sank home, and again, and yet again. Doggedly thrusting and withdrawing he continued along the line he had set for himself, and at the midway point of the wall's breadth, his blade met resistance. The tip of it grated against metal, slid off it, and penetrated wood.

His heart leaping with new triumph, Jamie withdrew the blade and inserted it again, probing inch by inch till it slid cleanly through with no resistance of either earth or wood to penetrate. This, then, was the point at which the wood behind the turf began!

He stood for a moment calculating the implications of his find. If the bank was, in actual fact, a concealment for the entrance to the tunnel, the wood his sword had found was probably a door. The point at which his sword had slid through into space must be the jamb on one side of that door, and somewhere down the line of that jamb or its equivalent on the door's other side, there must be a spring or a lock or a catch of some kind.

Fingers shaking now with excitement, he probed a few inches beneath the protruding sword-hilt. His fingers touched a knob of metal. It moved in his grip and he heard a faint click. Still holding on to the knob, he pulled sharply. A section of the wall came swinging towards him, the blades of the turf over-planted on the wood of it disentangling reluctantly from the rest of the grass around.

Released by the opening door his sword fell with a soft thump at his feet. He picked it up, then pushing the door open to its widest extent, he kicked a bundle of reeds together and wedged them firmly under it. There was no wind and so it was unlikely the door would blow shut by accident. All the same, it was just as well to be sure it would be wide open for him if and when he had to make a retreat!

He straightened up with a mixture of emotions gripping him — elation, fear, curiosity, and a sudden feeling of guilt that his intended actions would lead to danger for Marie. Impatiently he pushed the guilty feelings down. She was not the fragile doll her father took her to be, he told himself. Neither was she the delicate miss of Macey's imagination. She was a courageous, resourceful girl — and just as foolhardy as himself when it came to the pinch!

"*Danger makes me happy*" — that was what she had said! And smiling to himself in the darkness at the brave ring of the remembered words, Jamie stepped boldly into the passage behind the door.

12. *Trapped!*

He was in a tunnel, stone-paved underfoot, the walls on either side shored with timbers. A few steps from the open doorway and the grey glimmer from the outside world vanished. The tunnel became pitch-black so that it was impossible to judge distance except by counting his paces. Silently he began to do so and with finger-tips guiding him on either side moved blindly forward.

It was a more difficult thing to do than he had imagined. The darkness pressed in on him chokingly, almost as if he were being forced to breathe the stuff of which it was made. The click of his hesitant steps on the paved floor was thrown back by the tunnel walls, echoing like the footsteps of some stealthy pursuer who stopped when he stopped, pursued again when he moved on. And so it continued for two hundred nerve-racking paces.

At the end of that time he was brought up abruptly against a solid wall. He ran his fingers over it. It was of wood, smoothly grained apart from a carved centre panel. There was no opening in the wood, no lock, no latch of any kind. Defeated, Jamie's hands dropped to his sides and he was almost on the point of turning away when a sudden thought struck him.

Why should there be a carved panel in the blank end-wall of a hidden tunnel?

Curiously he felt over the raised outline of the wooden design. His fingers traced a pattern of fleur-de-lis. "Lilies," he muttered, "— the lilies of France," and rapidly his mind made the connecting links. The fleur-de-lis was the royal emblem of France. The tunnel gave secret access to the palace of the old French queen. Where better then could the key to it be hidden than in this carving of the fleur-de-lis?

Once again he felt the carving, his fingers pressing purposefully this time at every leaf and petal, and this time he found the vital spot. As he touched the base of the central petal in the design the wall trembled. It yielded under the pressure of his fingers and became a door that swung slowly away from him to settle soundlessly back on hidden hinges. As it swung Jamie unsheathed his sword and stood tensely on guard. Light washed feebly into the tunnel from the space beyond the door but no sound followed its opening, no cry of warning or alarm. Cautiously he moved forward to peer round the door and found himself looking down the vista of a long, low-raftered wine cellar.

It was an eerie place. The lamp that had shone into the tunnel hung from one of the rafters but its light was too dim to penetrate into the furthest reaches of the cellar. Great shadows lurked there. Great pyramids of barrels loomed out of them, and other barrels were scattered in twos and threes over the wide expanse of floor between him and the opposite wall.

There was another door there. He could just see its outline facing him in the lamp's feeble light, but to reach it he would have to brave the menace of the shadows lurking between the barrels. And each of them was big enough to conceal more than one crouching assailant!

Skin prickling with awareness of danger, Jamie moved out across the floor, every moment expecting the shadows to leap into sudden violent life. The eerie silence held. Step by crouching step he reached the door at last and, reassured by having come thus far in safety, sheathed his sword again.

The door that faced him now was a massive structure of wood thickly studded with great iron nails. Evidently it was the main entrance to the cellar and he was not surprised, therefore, to find it locked fast. Perfunctorily he tried the latch and when the door did not yield looked around frowning over the problem of exit from the cellar.

This great wooden door, he reasoned, would be the one used by those who had legitimate business in the cellar. But for those who entered it secretly by means of the tunnel there must be another exit into the palace, and most probably one that was concealed by a device similar to that controlling the tunnel door. And on this conclusion he began to move rapidly along the panelled wall, fingers probing, eyes peering for a repetition of the fleur-de-lis carving.

He found it eventually at the far end of the wall to the right of the door by which he had entered the cellar. Once again he pressed firmly at the base of the centre petal, and once again a section of the wall swung at the command of a hidden mechanism. The door that opened swung inwards to the cellar as the other had done, but no light followed on its opening. It was only the light spilling from the cellar that showed him what lay behind the second door.

A stone wall faced him. There was only about two feet between it and the wall of the cellar itself, and in this narrow space was the beginning of a flight of steps leading upwards. Beyond that he could not see for the stairs turned in a spiral and cautiously mounting to the first twist of this spiral he peered ahead. A blank wall of darkness faced him for the cellar light was cut off by this turn in the stairs. Curiosity was stronger now, however, than any fear of the trap this narrow space might represent, and he kept mounting slowly upwards. The stairs twisted again, and at this second twist in the spiral his fingers sliding along the smooth stone of the wall on his left came into contact with yet another carving of the fleur-de-lis design.

For a moment or two then, Jamie hesitated. The spiral of the stairs wound still further ahead of him and he was impatient to find where they led, but prudence warned him that this repeated design of the fleur-de-lis should be investigated before he committed himself to the rest of the ascent. Prudence won the battle in his mind. He fumbled over the carving, found the central petal, and pressed against it. The solid stone yielded to his touch as easily as the wood of the cellar had done and the darkness of the stairs lightened to grey with the noiseless opening of yet another secret door.

Warily Jamie stepped through the space it left and saw that the greyish light filtering into the stairs came from two narrow slits of windows, one on either side of a tall, Gothic-arched door. The door was set in a wall to his left and on his right was the first flight of another spiral staircase winding round the massive support of a central stone column.

It was too dim to see anything else but there was a sense of space above and ahead of him. The size of the door and the broad sweep of the stairs were further signs of a spacious apartment, and together they indicated that he was standing in the hallway of the main entrance to the palace. The fact that the stairs wound round a central support meant that they were housed in a tower abutting on the main building, and from this it could be presumed that there were landings at the various floor levels each providing access to the rooms on that floor.

It was a common style of building and therefore easily guessed at. It took several minutes longer, however, to place the narrow stair and the secret door in relation to it but the significance of their position struck Jamie eventually. Glancing from the narrow to the broad spiral of stairs, he realized that the wall of the tower was hollow, with the space between the inner and the outer walls housing the narrow stair and the secret door providing access between the two.

In effect, he had discovered the way in which entry could be secretly obtained either to the public part of the palace or to whatever room or rooms could be reached by the stairway hidden in the tower's hollow wall. But which stairway was the one more likely to lead him to where Marie was hidden?

Almost certainly the secret stairway, he decided. But he could not risk mounting it till he had closed the connecting door between the two. The enemy might be in occupation of the palace and if this was so the discovery of an open door would point immediately to the presence of an intruder.

Quickly stepping back on to the narrow stair Jamie grasped the ridged outline of the fleur-de-lis with his finger-tips. To his relief the door swung easily towards him. It closed as soundlessly as it had opened and smoothly fitted back into place again. Once more he was wrapped in darkness and blindly feeling his way again he continued his ascent of the secret stair.

The spiral wound in wide curves which he guessed would cross the broad inner spiral at points between the various floor levels of the tower, and it continued so narrow that his hands guiding him on either side were pressed close to his shoulders. Still he mounted steadily upwards, turn after turn of the spiral dropping behind him. There was no break in the smoothness of the wall on either side, no window-slit, no outline of a door, but the height he had climbed warned him eventually that he must be near the top of the building.

It was with this thought in his mind that his left hand brushed over another carving of the now-familiar fleur-de-lis design. He stopped, but almost immediately moved on again with the quick realisation that another secret door in the left-hand wall of the stairway could only lead on, as the one at the foot of the stair had done, to the public part of the palace. Another turn of the narrow stairs and this time he was halted by a wooden door facing him. He reached above his head and his finger-tips grazed a ceiling. He had arrived at the head of the secret stair.

The door in front of him was polished and smooth. His hands slid over it gropingly and with a thrill of triumph he felt the outline of a lock with a key inserted in it. Gently, holding it in both hands to check any sudden click, he turned the key. The wards were oiled. They slipped smoothly back and the door was open.

As carefully then as he had turned the key, Jamie eased his sword from its scabbard. When it was free, he pushed the door inch by inch away from him. A panelled wall came into view on his right. It was close enough to touch with his hand and there was light palely reflected on it from somewhere in the room. No sound reached him and now the door was open wide enough for him to peer round its edge. He did so, with infinite caution. The room was long and low with only a few pieces of necessary furniture in it. All this he took in at a glance, and then at the far end of the room he saw Marie Forbes.

She was half-sitting, half-lying on the floor, her body partly supported by a low stool. Her left arm was thrown back over this stool, her right arm drooped down by her side, and on her face upturned to the candlelight there was the stillness and pallor of death.

A gasp of horror rose to Jamie's lips and without even being aware that he had moved he was across the floor and kneeling by her side. For a long agonized minute he stared at the waxen face and closed eyes, not daring the touch that would confirm his fears, then reaching out a shaking hand he laid the tips of his fingers against her neck. Her skin was warm. His fingers sought the pulse at her throat and with a quick, indrawn breath he felt its uncertain beat. Far gone as she was, Marie was still alive.

Gently he lifted the arm that lay by her side. The wine cup held loosely between her fingers dropped to the floor. Her eyelids fluttered and opened slowly and she stared blankly at him.

"'Tis Jamie — Jamie Morton the caddie," he whispered reassuringly, and smiled at her.

Her eyes took on life as she recognized him. Her lips move, but no words came. Again she tried to speak and this time he caught the whisper:

"*The wine ... d'Aquirre ... poison ... in the wine ...*"

Her eyelids fluttered and drooped again and with renewed horror gripping him at her whispered words Jamie stared down at the wine cup that had fallen from her fingers. There were dregs still in it and spreading across the floor where she lay there was a trail of the liquid.

The same wine that had been in the cup? If so, how much of it had been spilt? How much of the poisoned stuff had she drunk?

In a rush of panic Jamie seized the girl by the shoulders and jerked her sitting upright. "*How much? How much poison have you drunk?*" he whispered fiercely.

Her eyes flew open and stared at him, bright now

with tears and terror, and in their look he read the answer he had dreaded.

Without further ado he raised her to her feet. Flinging one of her arms round his neck he gripped it firmly, supporting her round the waist with his other arm.

"I shall take your weight as much as I can," he whispered, "but you must move your feet forward, Mistress Marie."

She lolled against him, apparently unable to support herself. Patiently he placed her on her feet again and with his face close to hers whispered urgently: "Walk if you want to live, Mistress Marie! I am taking you home. Walk!"

The words seemed to penetrate. Her limp form straightened and she took a stumbling step along with him. Another step, and another, and Jamie began to believe that they might reach the door. He looked up to judge the distance they would have to cross to reach it and with a shock of dismay that froze him in mid-step saw the tall black figure of d'Aquirre framed in the opening.

The man in black stepped slowly forward his long face twisted in astonished disdain, and halting in front of Jamie and Marie he said contemptuously:

"So it was *you* I heard moving about up here!"

Jamie continued to stand dumbly supporting Marie's sagging body. His mind was terrifyingly blank of any initiative and it was like a person trapped in a nightmare that he heard d'Aquirre continue:

"You are very young to seek death so eagerly, but nevertheless, I can accommodate you! It may take an hour or so to summon the means of course, but this will give you time to meditate the folly of your actions — particularly as the young woman herself will be dead before your turn comes!"

It was the indescribable malice in the sound of the final words that shocked Jamie's numb mind into action. A whole world of thought flashed through his brain at lightning speed. D'Aquirre's character unfolded itself — the coldness, the cruelty, the aristocratic hauteur that would not stoop to offer violence to a lowly creature like himself but would disdainfully pass on the task to some hired assassin. He saw Marie lying dead in this dim, secret room, himself waiting helplessly for the murderer's knife-thrust and this loathsome creature in front of him striding free from his hiding place to spread havoc and war throughout the land.

He glared at d'Aquirre standing waiting as if in malicious expectation of some plea for mercy. It must not be — it *would* not be, he vowed silently. Somehow he would make d'Aquirre himself stand and fight. It was their only hope. In a voice that lashed like a whip he said:

"I would rather a thousand times die the creature I am than live for an hour the rotten copy of a man that you are!"

D'Aquirre's face twitched at the insult then he smiled his thin-lipped caricature of mirth. "That gutter tongue of yours is too long," he sneered. "'Tis high time your throat was cut."

He turned on his heel and at his movement Jamie swiftly unhooked Marie's arm from his neck. She staggered back towards the stool and collapsed against it as he drew his sword shouting:

"Turn and fight, d'Aquirre! Or are you too much the coward?"

D'Aquirre only paused long enough to glance at the blade in his hand, and striding again to the door threw disdainfully over his shoulder:

"Do you expect me to soil my hands with garbage?"

He reached the door with the words but as his hand went out to the latch Jamie hurled his sword forward with all his strength behind the gesture. Sensing the danger, d'Aquirre whipped round in time to avoid the whirling blade. He staggered against the door and it banged shut with the impact of his body against it. Jamie was already charging forward, his head lowered to butt into d'Aquirre's chest as he backed, spread-eagled, against the door. The man in black doubled up gasping, and swiftly retreating a step, Jamie bent to recover his sword.

D'Aquirre's foot shot out and sent it spinning but he was still too winded to put much force into the gesture. Before he could straighten up again and pull the door open to make his exit Jamie had swooped to recover the sword, and with rage contorting his features, d'Aquirre drew his own blade. They faced one another and the rage in d'Aquirre's face brought vividly to Jamie's mind the warning Forbes had once given him:

"*Never let anger rule you while the sword is in your hand.*"

The recollection effectively cooled his own rage so that he met the other's first savage lunge steadily. His blade crossed d'Aquirre's in a ringing blow, and for the first few moments with his antagonist pinned to the door and still breathless, he had the advantage. Then the man in black broke free of the door and circling for position brought into play the long reach his height afforded him. Momentarily Jamie had need of all his agility to keep out of range of the long-reaching blade but his confidence remained unshaken for the few minutes' engagement had shown him the truth of the comment Forbes had made about d'Aquirre. He *was* an indifferent swordsman!

All he had to do, Jamie calculated exultantly, was to rob d'Aquirre of the advantage of his height by keeping the battle mobile. Thus, with freedom to manoeuvre, he could seize the moment when his superior skill would allow him to press rapidly in under d'Aquirre's weak guard and strike the decisive blow.

Coldly he planned for the moment, fighting defensively, retreating and circling to take up a new position, each retreat and re-engagement forcing d'Aquirre to a change of stroke and re-arrangement of balance that obviously taxed his limited skill.

The battle had carried them now over to the far side of the room where the candlelight fell brightest. D'Aquirre was backing, his strokes falling wilder and slower. The moment was almost come, Jamie decided, and positioned himself for the final sortie. One lightning glance took in the corner of the room, the stool, the guttering candle, Marie's still form huddled against the wall, and in a spasm of wild hatred for d'Aquirre, he lunged.

Too late he remembered the pool of spilt wine by the stool. His right foot advancing for the lunge slid across the wet floor and slipped sideways. Panic flashing up he checked the lunge and leapt back, but only into fresh disaster. One foot landed on the rounded edge of the wine cup lying on the floor and his balance went completely.

Feet flying from under him, Jamie crashed to the ground. The back of his head struck against the wall in a blow that sent blinding pain across his brow. The darkness of unconsciousness rushed over his mind, drowning the pain, but for a fraction of a second before his senses went he was aware of a tall black figure advancing towards him, sword in hand. The sword flashed as d'Aquirre raised it, then mercifully the darkness claimed him completely and blotted out the sight of the descending death-stroke.

13. *A Find and a Chase*

From somewhere very far away a voice was calling his name insistently, "*Jamie! Jamie! Jamie!*"

The voice woke the pain in his head again. It stabbed across his brow and he groaned. His eyelids fluttered in protest and the voice, now loud and close to him, said:

"He is coming back to his senses."

Jamie's eyes flew open and met Tod's anxious face bent over him. The rest of the room was hidden by his body and Jamie rolled his head to try and see beyond him.

"D'Aquirre...?" he muttered. "Where is he?"

"D'Aquirre is dead. Look!"

Tod raised him into a sitting position and pointed with his free hand. The room swam in a blur of objects in front of Jamie's eyes. He blinked to clear his vision and everything sprang suddenly into focus. D'Aquirre lay a yard from him in a tumbled heap of sprawling black limbs, the agony of death frozen on his contorted face. The Cleek stood over the body, his wrinkled face set in lines of grim satisfaction. And in the corner by the stool and the trickle of spilt wine Macey knelt with the limp form of Marie Forbes in the crook of his arm.

As Jamie sat up he looked over her head at the Cleek and said quietly, "She lives yet — but not for long unless I can take her to skilled help for her condition."

He gathered her into his arms and rising to his feet nodded at d'Aquirre's body. "Search him, Cleek. Tod, you will escort me as far as the lochside and then return here with my further instructions."

Tod followed him as he strode rapidly out and the Cleek bent to the task assigned to him. Jamie watched him for a few moments then rising cautiously to his feet he tried his strength. His head was still throbbing but apart from that he had suffered no harm and when the first dizziness brought on by his change in position had subsided he turned back to the Cleek.

The old man was examining the articles he had found on d'Aquirre. They were few enough — a gold comfit-box with some lozenges in it, a fine lawn handkerchief edged with lace, and a small leather pouch containing a handful of gold and silver coins. There were no letters, no papers of any kind.

Replacing the coins in the bag the Cleek pushed the articles aside with a grunt of disgust and looked Jamie critically up and down.

"You had better rest while you can," he advised. "That was a sore dunt on the head you took when you fell."

Tenderly Jamie felt the swelling on the back of his head, wincing as his fingers touched it. "What happened?" he asked. "How came you all to the palace — and who was it killed d'Aquirre?"

"You have Macey to thank for that last mercy." The Cleek rose and came over to him. "Lucky for you, my lad, that old Cleek is a light sleeper! You were not long gone when I woke — your mattress was still warm to the touch."

Jamie flushed under the glare that accompanied this comment but he had the wisdom to keep his silence and the Cleek went on, "I thought you had gone to Forbes's house and so Tod and I hurried there first, wondering all the time, I may tell you, how we could evade the guard round it. But here was a curious thing, Jamie. There were no guards there! There was not a soul to be seen except Macey himself and he, it seemed, had already discovered that the guards had been withdrawn and was preparing to take advantage of their absence. He was in the act of leaving the house as we came up and when he said he had not seen you that night I guessed you must have gone by yourself to look for the secret entrance to the palace."

"So you found the door into the tunnel then?" Jamie ventured.

"Lucky again for you that you had the sense to leave it open behind you," the Cleek nodded. "As it was, we only arrived in the nick of time. D'Aquirre was standing over you like an executioner when we came through that door, but Macey rushed in so quick to the attack that the villain had scarce time to realize we were there before he was run through."

He glanced distastefully at the body then moved away to sit on a wooden settle near the door. A gesture of his cleek commanded Jamie to share the seat. "You have had rare good luck tonight, Jamie," he said thoughtfully, "and for all your headstrong ways you have aquitted yourself well. I am proud of you, lad."

Praise from the Cleek was praise indeed and Jamie flushed with pleasure at his words. A feeling of exhilaration swept over him with the full realisation of the success that had crowned his rash efforts to find Marie and he was suddenly eager for further action. The night's events were not over yet, after all, if Macey's parting words were any guide.

With mounting impatience he listened for Tod's returning step on the stair outside. It came at last. The Cleek struggled up with him as he jumped to his feet and together they greeted the big man with an eager, "What now, Tod?"

"Macey thinks d'Aquirre must have had a hiding

place in some other part of the palace," Tod announced. "We are to seek it out while he takes the girl to her home."

"I know the way into the main part of the palace!" Jamie exclaimed. "I discovered it on my way to this room."

"So you made even better use of your time than I gave you credit for," the Cleek commented. He gave a brief cackle of amusement then turning back to Tod demanded, "Does Macey hope to find the Spanish Letters in d'Aquirre's hiding place?"

"Aye, he thinks they may be hidden there," Tod said. "I told him of course that none of us could read but he said 'twas no matter. We are to collect every document we can find for him to examine."

Jamie reached up as Tod spoke and took the candle from its sconce on the wall. "This will light us to begin with," he said, "and maybe we will find others as we go."

He made for the secret stair, Tod and the Cleek closely following, and at the end of the first downward flight held the candle high so that its beam fell on the fleur-de-lis carving he had passed without examining on his way up.

"Now watch," he told the other two, and pressed at the base of the centre petal. Murmurs of astonishment broke from them at his guess at the existence of a door corresponding to the one at the foot of the stair was proved correct. Jamie led the way through it and on to the landing beyond.

"We are on a landing of the main stairway in the palace," he explained, and holding the candle so that it lit the steps below them he went on to describe the secret of the tower's hollow wall.

"A most cunning arrangement," the Cleek commented. He reached for the candle and swung it round to examine the landing. The light fell on a door facing the one they had just come through and he hobbled briskly towards it. Pushing it open he said over his shoulder, "We might as well look here first for fresh candles."

He stepped into the room with the candle held aloft but checked again almost immediately. Jamie and Tod were brought up short behind him on the threshold and in silence all three surveyed the interior revealed by the candlelight.

The room had evidently been lived in for somc timc and there were still traces of recent occupation. A small table bore the remains of a meal. In one corner there was a bundle of candles and a further store of food and wine. A camp-bed with neatly-folded bedding stood against one wall and on a chair by a writing desk lay a black velvet cloak and a high-crowned black hat.

On the desk itself stood a small black leather valise and as soon as his eyes lit on this Jamie pushed his way past the Cleek. The valise resembled exactly in size and shape the one in which Sempill had carried the gold to the tinsmith's house and Jamie reached for it eagerly. A gasp of astonishment at its weight escaped him. Abruptly he set it down again and turned to find the Cleek at his elbow.

"Is it locked?" the old man asked. He waited while Jamie tried the clasp and found it firm then gave the candle to him to hold while he picked up the heavy iron poker lying in the hearth of the fireplace. Jamie watched him fearfully.

"'Twill be a hanging matter if you break it open," he protested.

"'Tis a hanging matter for us to be here at all!" the Cleek told him scornfully, and raising the poker he brought it down heavily on the lock of the valise.

Two more blows were needed before the lock was smashed. At the third one the valise opened slightly. The Cleek prised its sides apart and even although Jamie had guessed what the contents would be he still could not suppress an exclamation at the glitter of the gold that lay revealed. Bright and hard and yellow as sunshine the Spanish doubloons, crowns, and pistolets winked up at him, their hard-packed glitter filling the valise to the brim.

The Cleek also drew a long breath of wonder at the sight. His eyes met Jamie's in a glance of mutual triumph but almost immediately his expression altered and he asked slowly:

"Jamie, how did d'Aquirre know you were in the secret room?"

"He said he heard me moving about," Jamie told him.

He glanced to the door then up to the ceiling, quickly working out their position in relation to the room where he had found Marie. They were directly below it, he realized, and pointed this out to the Cleek.

"Aye, but the sound you made did not waken him," the old man said, "for this bed has not been slept in tonight. Moreover, he was fully dressed except for his hat and cloak — and here *they* are all ready laid out to wear."

Speaking half to himself he went on, "The guard withdrawn from Forbes's house — d'Aquirre fully dressed at this hour of the night — his hiding place all tidy except for this recent meal — the girl disposed of and the gold ready to carry away —"

"He was preparing to leave quietly — suddenly, without us or anyone else being aware of it," Jamie concluded for him.

"Leaving the girl alone upstairs to die a slow death from poison!"

Tod's voice, so seldom heard but shaking now with some strong emotion, broke in and brought them both round to face him. He was standing watching them with his head lowered and shoulders hunched like some great animal at bay, his huge hands clenched into fists, the veins on his temples tensed and swollen. Tod was in a rage — one of those rare but merciless rages that seized him when he was faced with some act of brutality towards a helpless creature.

D'Aquirre's crime against Marie Forbes was just such an act, Jamie thought. It was this that has roused Tod and a tremor of apprehension ran over him at the prospect of the rough justice the big man would deal to any accomplice of d'Aquirre's unlucky enough to fall into his hands. The Cleek, however, did not allow the tension of the moment to grow.

"We are wasting time," he said sharply. "Light some of those candles and start searching for the letters."

Setting an example to the other two he took a candle from d'Aquirre's store and lit it from the stump that Jamie held. Tod followed suit without any further reference to Marie, and when Jamie had also lit a fresh candle they began the search. The Cleek took the writing-desk, Jamie the bed, and Tod the chimney-piece. From these they progressed to a minute examination of the floor and the panelled walls, methodically tapping for hollow places and loose boards. They searched the hat and cloak, ripped the stuffing from the seat of the chair and the down from the pillow on the bed, but in the end all they had found for their labours was a few charred fragments of paper at the back of the fireplace.

"D'Aquirre has been too clever for us it seems," Jamie said disconsolately.

No one had anything to add to this and a dismal

silence ensued — a silence that was broken with startling effect by the sound of footsteps on the secret stair. Instantly the Cleek nipped out the flame of his candle.

"It could be Macey returning," Tod whispered.

"Put out your candles — it could be *anyone!*" the Cleek whispered fiercely in return.

Jamie and Tod obeyed. The steps reached the fleur-de-lis door in the stairway wall. They halted there, and Jamie suddenly remembered that they had left this door open behind them. The halt was only momentary, however. The footsteps went on, fading from hearing as they ascended to the wooden door. Silence for a few moments, then faintly overheard they heard the intruder crossing the floor of the secret room.

"Get behind the door, Tod," the Cleek said quietly. "Be ready to leap out and waylay him when he comes down if he refuses to declare himself."

Tod glided across the room to take up position behind the door and the Cleek pulled Jamie crouching down with behind the writing desk. The intruder was now re-tracing his steps across the secret room and a few seconds later they heard him descending the stairs. Once again he halted at the fleur-de-lis doorway, and this time it was a much longer pause. Jamie held his breath and in the silence it seemed fantastically as if all the ghosts of the great empty building beneath were listening with him.

Slowly the strange footsteps crossed the landing between the stair and d'Aquirre's room. They halted at the threshold. Crouching forward on hands and knees Jamie strained to identify the man standing there but even though his eyes were now accustomed to the gloom he could make out no distinguishing feature of the dark bulk in the doorway. The intruder sniffed, apparently scenting the tallow-smell left in the air by the recently-doused candles and the Cleek said quietly:

"Macey?"

A startled exclamation broke from the man in the doorway at the sound. He turned to run, and simultaneously Tod launched himself from hiding. His leap fell short. He crashed to the ground but almost immediately was on his feet again. Jamie leapt from hiding as he rose.

"Down the main stair, Tod!" he yelled. "Down the main stair and we can head him off from the cellar!" But deaf to his shouts Tod rushed to follow the intruder's line of flight down the secret stairway and Jamie plunged forward himself down the main stairs.

As he thundered down the winding steps he heard the Cleek's feet clattering behind him and the sound of his voice railing at the folly of such a rapid descent in the darkness but he shut his ears to the old man's warning cries. The secret stairway was so much narrower than the main stair that neither Tod nor the man he pursued could hope to descend as quickly to ground level as he was doing. But he had still to open the doorway between the front hall and the narrow stair and this might yet consume the vital seconds needed to cut the fugitive off from the cellar!

With his shoulders buffeting the wall at every twist of the spiral yet still by some miracle of balance keeping his feet in the downward rush, Jamie reached the last turn and saw the outer doorway of the hall ahead. A flying leap carried him over the last dozen steps. He landed on hands and knees, and breathlessly reaching up slid his hands over the wall. His fingers touched a fleur-de-lis carving. He pressed against it, scrambling to his feet to allow the secret door to swing back. Nothing happened. Impatiently he pressed again but still the wall did not move. Puzzled, he felt on either side of the carving and the cold sweat started out on his brow as his fingers encountered a continuous fresco of the fleur-de-lis motif carved along the wall of the hall-way.

Feverishly he tried to recall the exact position in which he had stood on his first entrance into the hall-way, but even as he did so he realized that the difference of a mere two or three feet would involved several of these carvings. There was nothing for it but to experiment till he had found the right one and with a glum acceptance that his lead would vanish in the process he set about working his way along the line of carvings.

It was at the eighth try that he felt the familiar shudder of the stones under his hand. The hidden mechanism went into action and his heart beating high again with renewed hope Jamie stood aside to allow the concealed doorway to swing open. A space yawned in front of him and the sound of footsteps rapidly descending the secret stair broke thunderously on his hearing.

A figure crouched and running hard flashed past him. He plunged in pursuit, conscious as he did so of other steps still descending the stairs above him, and emerging into the cellar with a rush saw the man in front throw a rapid backward glance at him.

"*Sempill!*" he yelled, half in excited recognition and half in the vain hope that Sempill would turn and stand his ground, but Sempill did not check his flight across the cellar. Weaving and twisting between the barrels that littered the floor he ran for the open doorway marking the entrance to the tunnel, and despairingly aware that he was as good as free if he gained this doorway Jamie followed with all the speed he could muster.

He was halfway across the broad expanse of the cellar floor and Sempill was only a few yards from the door when something happened that changed the whole current of events. Macey appeared in the doorway to the tunnel. He blocked Sempill's way, sword in hand. Sempill slid to a halt, his sword flashing out to meet the challenge. In the same moment, Jamie felt himself being roughly thrust aside. It was Tod, shouldering his way past to advance on Sempill, hands outstretched, body bent in a wrestler's crouch.

"Stick him, Mr Macey!" he shouted savagely. "I will pin him from behind!"

Sempill's head swung warily from one man to the other, then suddenly he turned to the right and ran, away from both entrances into the cellar. Tod followed him like a hound slipped from its leash and in a flash Jamie had grasped the meaning of this new strategy. Caught between Tod and Macey, Sempill had no chance. But by drawing the unarmed Tod away from the doorway he could deal with him separately, for Macey would not dare risk deserting his guard over the only escape route from the cellar.

Unheeding Macey's shout to him to stand clear, Jamie leapt after the two men. Tod's pursuit had now developed into a ghastly game of tag with Sempill in which his aim was to force the other man into one of the confined spaces between the barrels and Sempill's was to remain on the open floor where he had freedom to use his sword. Unnoticed by either of them Jamie hovered on the outskirts of the chase, his sword ready to intervene at the first opportunity. The moment came as Sempill, pressed hard by Tod, turned to leap for the open space beyond the next group of barrels. With a running jump he cleared a row of wine flasks landing crouched almost at Jamie's feet.

Jamie struck. Sempill took the blow on his blade as he rose from the floor. The jarring force of his parry shuddered up Jamie's sword-arm so that his riposte was feeble and badly-judged. Realising this, he tried rapidly to disengage. A searing pain shot through his right shoulder and he reeled back from the thrust Sempill had dealt him, his sword drooping from a suddenly nerveless hand.

In a blur of pain and mortification at his failure, he was aware of Tod and Sempill circling like two snarling dogs in the cleared space beyond the barrels and then of the Cleek standing on the far side of them and yelling hoarsely. The old man swung suddenly sideways to the other two. His arm rose with the movement and the cleek in his hand when whirling towards Sempill. It spun across the floor at knee-level and struck Sempill's shin, clattered to the ground and caught between his feet. He tripped, clutching wildly at the air, and Tod launched himself like a thunderbolt.

They crashed to the ground with Sempill falling backwards and Tod's left hand grasping his right wrist, forcing the hand holding the sword back against the floor. Jamie staggered forward with the intention of seizing the sword while Sempill's wrist was pinned, and was halted in his tracks by the sickening sound of breaking bone as Sempill's wrist gave way under the pressure on it. The sword-blade tinkled on to the stone floor and with his one good hand Sempill clawed frantically at the grip Tod swiftly transferred to his throat.

The rage contorting the big man's face showed clearly that he had passed the point of reason where his victim was concerned and a surge of protest rose in Jamie at the sight. Quite apart from Sempill's value as a source of information it was impossible to stand by and watch the murder of a wounded man, and forgetting his own wound in the urgency of the moment he heaved frantically at Tod's shoulder. The Cleek, still yelling hoarsely, joined him in the struggle. Together they shouted and heaved as they tried to prise Tod away, but it was Macey's voice cutting through the din that penetrated the big man's maddened mind.

His shoulders suddenly relaxed and he rose slowly, hands dangling at his sides, chest heaving. Still dazed with his efforts Jamie also staggered to his feet.

"You — you almost choked him!" he spluttered.

The savage flame leapt again in Tod's eyes. His big hands began to rise again, crooked and threatening.

"You saw what they did to the girl," he growled, "a little helpless creature like her ..." The words trailed off in an inarticulate snarl and he would have pounced again on Sempill if Macey had not brought the flat of his sword smacking across his chest.

"*Stand back from the prisoner!*" His voice was a parade-ground roar that brought an element of sanity back to them all and obediently the three caddies fell back a few steps.

"Make your report," Macey snapped.

"We found d'Aquirre's hiding place and we searched it thoroughly," the Cleek said. "We found no trace of the Spanish Letters. But we did find the gold d'Aquirre got from Sempill."

"Where is it?"

The Cleek hobbled back to the place from which he had tossed his club and picked up the valise. Holding it open so that Macey could see the coins, he suggested, "I could lodge it with Heriot, the king's jeweller, for safe keeping."

Macey nodded a curt acknowledgement. "It will accrue as treasure trove to the Scottish crown in any case once this affair is settled," he added.

Sempill had begun to rise from the floor and bending down he jerked him roughly upright. "I will give you one chance to tell me the whereabouts of the correspondence between the Catholic conspirators in Scotland and the Spanish king," he said. "Speak now, Sempill, or take the consequences your actions have earned for you."

Nursing his broken right wrist in his left hand, Sempill looked slowly up at Macey's menacing face. His own face was white and his eyes were dimmed by the evident pain of his broken bones. Almost it looked, Jamie thought hopefully, as if he might yield at last, but apparently it took more than pain and defeat to break Sempill's will. He straightened himself, his expression hardening into lines of obstinacy as he replied:

"I have nothing to tell you."

"Very well. Tod, twist his uninjured arm behind his back and walk with him," Macey directed. "Jamie and I will come behind you. You, Cleek, will follow with the gold. Pick up his sword, Jamie."

Jamie stooped to recover Sempill's sword and the little procession formed up.

"March!" Macey ordered.

"One moment!" Sempill looked back over his shoulder. "Where are you taking me?"

"I am taking you to the house of Master John Forbes," Macey told him.

"Forbes?" Sempill's pale face grew bleaker still as he whispered the name.

"You have had all the mercy you can expect from me, Sempill," Macey said coldly. "Now it is Forbes's turn to deal justice to you."

14. Rough Justice

They emerged from the mouth of the tunnel into the grey half-light of the winter dawn and it was only then that Macey noticed the blood seeping from the wound in Jamie's shoulder. A curt command brought them all to a halt and rolling up a sleeve of his doublet he wrenched off the broad cuff of his shirt. Folding the heavy linen into a pad he pressed it against the wound and tied it into position with a lace from the front of his shirt.

His face as he worked was bleak enough to forbid conversation and when Jamie ventured to enquire after Mistress Marie he said shortly, "'Tis still in the balance what will become of her," and then shut his lips firmly as if even that had been too much to reveal. Nothing else was said after that till he asked suddenly, "Where did you first surprise Sempill?" and when Jamie told how they had heard him moving about in the secret room he nodded once or twice as if the reply confirmed some thought in his own mind.

It was still too early in the morning for many people to be abroad and guarded as he was there was no opportunity for Sempill to make a break for freedom so that their party attracted only an occasional passing glance on the way to Fisher's Close. The door of Forbes's house stood open there but the close itself was deserted and they hurried across it to the shelter of the house. In the passage between the front door and the *salle d'armes* they heard the sound of voices and the hurried footsteps of several people coming from the upstairs part of the house but Macey ignored the sounds of anxious bustle and walked straight through to the *salle d'armes*.

Angus Mhor stood there, a solitary towering figure in the middle of the long room.

"He is expecting us," Macey said in a low voice to Jamie, and indeed there was a look of expectation about the red-haired giant. It was a look that made Jamie uneasy, however, for as they approached with Sempill the Highlander's lips drew back in a grin of wolfish pleasure and his hand went to the hilt of the massive sword by his side.

"No, Angus!" Macey checked the movement quickly. "He is not to be touched till Forbes comes. That was his order."

Angus Mhor scowled, but the mention of his master's order was enough to bring him to reluctant obedience and he contented himself by stepping forward to grasp the prisoner by the arm opposite to the one held by Tod. Sempill was a tall man but he was drooping with fatigue and pain. With Tod on the one side and Angus on the other he was dwarfed into sudden insignificance, and seeing him thus Jamie felt an unexpected twinge of compassion for him. But Sempill was an enemy, he reminded himself. Moreover, he could have had a hand in the poisoning of Marie, and hardening his heart against the pity prompted by the man's condition he joined Macey and the Cleek as they drew away from the group.

"Well now, Mr Macey," the Cleek was saying, "and what chance do you think the lassie has against the poison they gave her?"

"As to that," Macey said slowly, "much depends yet on what her father has achieved since I brought her home. It seems that this poison that was put in her wine is a drug that is used in small doses for inducing sleep, and Forbes, who had been accustomed to seeing it used for bringing a temporary relief to the wounded after battle, recognized its symptoms as soon as he saw her. I left him and the maid-servant working to bring her to her senses, and he told me that if she could be wakened and *kept* awake till the drug had been worked from her system, she would live."

He looked away from them to conceal the sudden twitching of his face and after a moment added in a low tone, "That is, always providing she had not swallowed too much of it in the first instance."

"Some of the wine was spilt from her cup," Jamie reminded him, and Macey nodded. "That is our only hope," he said. "After that there is nothing left to us but revenge."

He shot a look of hatred at Sempill drooping between his gigantic guards, and the Cleek said suddenly:

"You have maybe acted too hastily, Mr Macey. D'ye recall what Sempill said at the Anchor Inn that time we learned d'Aquirre had the girl captive? '*This is none of my doing*,' he said. '*I do not war on women.*'"

Macey rounded on him fiercely. "He knew where Marie was hidden — and he was d'Aquirre's accomplice!"

"That still does not mean he had a hand in the poisoning," the Cleek persisted. "Sempill is a soldier, lad, not a creeping murderer like d'Aquirre."

Macey set his lips in stubborn refusal to reply to this and after a moment's silence Jamie said, "You brought him back here for Master Forbes to —" He hesitated, and then on a questioning note finished, "— to kill?"

"I agreed with Forbes that he could have Sempill if I failed to make him tell me the whereabouts of the Spanish Letters," Macey said coldly. "He has refused to speak and so I can do nothing further with him. Forbes has a right to vengeance and what he does now is no affair of mine."

"He cannot fight for his life now," the Cleek pointed out, but Macey only retorted bitterly, "After what he has done to Marie he deserves to die!"

"Man, man, you have no *proof* of what he has done!" the Cleek exclaimed. "I tell you, Mr Macey, your concern for the lassie has warped your judgement."

Macey bit his lips uneasily. For the first time in their acquaintance Jamie thought he looked unsure of himself, but suddenly he seemed to make up his mind. With a gesture that beckoned Jamie and the Cleek to go with him he walked back to Sempill and shot the words at him.

"Forbes is going to kill you, Sempill! Tell me where the letters are and I will plead for you. I will even stand by your side against him if you can prove you have not harmed his daughter."

Sempill blinked at him from blood-shot eyes. "His daughter?" he repeated vaguely. "I know nothing of her." His face twisted in a sudden grimace of pain. He looked dazed for a moment then he recovered himself and said in a stronger voice, "I will not tell you anything, Macey. The letters are my winning card. Besides," he smiled faintly with the ghost of his old mockery, "I was always a lucky man and my luck may not have run out yet!"

"'Tis run out now, Sempill," Macey said quietly. He turned away and pointed to the doorway of the *salle d'armes*. "Here comes your Nemesis."

Every eye in the room followed the hand pointing to the fencing master framed in the doorway. He stood perfectly still for a few moments as if to emphasize the effect of his appearance, then with slow deliberate tread he advanced towards their group. Halting before

Sempill he raked him in leisurely fashion with his eyes and Sempill stiffened, flushing slowly under his gaze.

Jamie exchanged swift glances with the Cleek. This silence of Forbes was far more deadly than all his previous posturings and ravings, he thought, and the Cleek's expression showed that he shared this opinion. There was not a shred of hope left now for Sempill.

Forbes's first words confirmed their surmise. In a voice as cold as ice he said, "I am going to kill you, Sempill. Not, as I would have done once, in fair fight to avenge my brother's death, but in cold blood as an executioner would do. I am going to kill you for the attempted poisoning of my daughter."

Sempill gasped, seemingly utterly taken aback by this speech, but when Forbes reached for the sword that hung by his side he said urgently, "Forbes, I am ready to give you satisfaction for Neil's death, wounded as I am — but your daughter! I swear to heaven, man, that I am guiltless of any harm done to her!"

"Heaven cannot hear you," Forbes told him calmly, "and I have a nearer witness to your guilt in the girl's condition when they brought her to me."

He drew his sword and at the faint hiss of the steel sliding from its scabbard Sempill made a wild break to free himself.

"Hold him tight, Angus," Forbes said, still in his unnaturally calm voice, and Sempill shouted desperately, "I have not harmed her! Bring her here and she will tell you herself!"

Forbes raised his blade. He levelled it on Sempill's heart and for a second of horrified reality Jamie realized that the fencing master did indeed mean to kill Sempill in cold blood. Yet somehow he had no impulse to intervene as he had done against Tod's mad rage in the cellar.

Nor had any of the others apparently. Forbes's calm certainty that Sempill deserved to die seemed to have had the same hypnotic effect on them all.

His arm drew back. A line of light caught the moving blade and ran along its deadly length and suddenly Jamie found that he could not bear to watch the final action in the drama. With Sempill's repeated shout of "*Bring her here! Bring her here!*" ringing in his ears he turned abruptly away, only to be transfixed by the sight of Marie herself staggering into the room.

She was supported by the sturdy arms of Nan, the serving-maid, and it was Nan's voice shouting, "She is here, my masters, she *is* here!" that brought Forbes's head jerking round and the tip of his blade quivering to a halt only inches away from Sempill's heart. Locked together the girl and the woman bore down on him in a stumbling rush that brought Marie thrusting between him and Sempill.

"Leave him — he tried to save me!" she cried.

Pushing herself free of Nan's support she tried to speak again and failed, and would have fallen helplessly forward if Forbes had not caught her in his arms. Macey leapt to his aid with a shouted command that sent Jamie racing for a stool that stood in a corner amidst a clutter of fencing gear. When he returned with it to the confusion of talk that had broken out round Marie, the two men lowered her gently on to it. Forbes knelt in front of her, clasping her hands tightly in his. Macey knelt also, supporting her back with his arm. The talk died into silence as she opened her eyes again with a little shuddering sigh. Her gaze rested on Forbes's face upturned to hers and she repeated weakly:

"He tried to save me."

Forbes glanced uncomprehendingly from her to

Sempill. He was looking at Marie with a mixture of relief and bewilderment in his face, and when Forbes looked up he said uncertainly:

"Yes, I *did* try, but ..."

He hesitated, the air of bewilderment deepening on his face, and Macey said gently, "Tell us what happened, Mistress Marie. We *must* know."

"There was a knot-hole in the floor of the room," she began unsteadily. "I had my sewing scissors in my pocket when I was captured and I used them to work the knot out of the wood. I put my ear to the hole and in the room beneath I heard them — Sempill and d'Aquirre — talking of the plan to kill me."

She stopped, gasping for breath, and Sempill broke in, "It was d'Aquirre's plan and I told him I would have no hand in it. I —"

"Let her speak, Sempill!" Macey thundered, but Forbes chimed in angrily, "She is too weak to continue. Let *him* tell the story and she can either confirm or deny it."

"He is cunning enough to twist matters with clever words," Macey said implacably, "and she is in not state to argue the case with him. She must tell the story herself if we are to arrive at the truth."

"'Fore heaven, you are a hard man!"

The Cleek, silent for so long, startled them all with the exclamation he directed suddenly at Macey. Glaring at him in the hush his words had produced the old man added: "You act as if your heart was engaged to the lass and yet you show no heart or mercy for her in her weakness. What kind of loving is this, pray, that allows you to speak so harshly to her!"

Macey went white to the lips under this attack, but instead of replying directly to the Cleek he said quietly to Marie:

"'Tis not with my heart but with my mind and will that I must speak if I am to be faithful to the trust reposed in me."

She turned her head and eyed him steadily without replying, and pleadingly he added, "Believe me, Mistress, I would give all the world to let my heart speak for me now."

She smiled suddenly at his words and said, so softly that they scarcely heard her: "Yet can I hear it speak now above those other voices that command your loyalty!"

Her eyes held Macey's and at the look that passed between them it seemed to Jamie that the two of them were as good as promised to one another now. A glance at the Cleek caught him nodding with such satisfaction in the exchange provoked by his outburst that, in spite of the tenseness of the situation, he had to smother a laugh. Hastily he turned back to Marie. She had begun speaking again and though her words still came slowly the hesitation had vanished from her voice, and so she continued, unfaltering, to the end of her narrative.

"It was yesterday evening that I heard them speak," she said. "They were angry, shouting at one another so that their voices came clearly to me. D'Aquirre was insisting that it would be folly to leave anyone alive who could testify against them in the event of a failure of the rebellion, and as the argument proceeded I learned that he had given orders for the guard over our house to be withdrawn that night. This, he said, would lull you all into a false sense of safety. You would set out to look for me when I was not returned as he had promised and be secretly set upon and killed by men he would hire for that purpose.

"Colonel Sempill did not contest this part of the plan. It was d'Aquirre's proposal that I should be the first to be killed that roused him to wrath. He swore many oaths and told d'Aquirre that he would not war against women, and he threatened to kill him there and then if he did not keep his bargain to release me unharmed. I could tell from d'Aquirre's voice that he was afraid Colonel Sempill would carry out his threat and he agreed at last that he would not harm me."

Marie paused at this point and looked intently at her father. Then speaking to him alone, she continued, "Before he left the palace Sempill told d'Aquirre that he would return at first light today to see that I was released as promised, and he repeated his threat to kill d'Aquirre if any harm came to me before then. So you see, Papa, he did not try to kill me. He did his best to save my life."

Forbes dropped his gaze from hers and bowed his head on to their clasped hands. "Go on, daughter," he muttered.

Marie looked compassionately down at the bowed head and freeing one hand she rested it gently on his thick, iron-grey hair. "The wine d'Aquirre brought with my supper tray was poisoned," she said simply. "I drank half of it before I tasted the bitterness of the drug he had mixed with it. I put the cup down then, and tried to be calm. Later on I remember I picked it up again meaning to empty the rest of the wine from it for fear he should return and force me to drink it. But by that time the poison had begun to take effect on me. I remember falling from the stool where I sat with the cup in my hand and after that I knew nothing more till I heard Jamie's voice speaking to me."

Slowly Forbes rose to his feet. With bent head he walked to the far end of the *salle d'armes* and paused there with his back to them and his head still bent in thought. Marie drooped tiredly on her stool and Macey whispered something to her. She smiled and nodded and he drew her gently back to rest against his shoulder. Forbes turned and walked back to them. His face was expressionless, his tone when he spoke to Sempill was cold and formal.

"I believe my daughter's statement that you tried to save her life," he said, "therefore there are no more scores to settle between us. You have paid the debt you owed me for my brother's death at Liège and you may leave my house in freedom."

Sempill gave a long sigh of relief. "If you would instruct your guards to loose me ..." he suggested.

Forbes raised his hand in a gesture of dismissal to Tod and Angus but with a cry of "Hold!" Macey was on his feet.

"You are losing sight of the main purpose," he told Forbes curtly, and swung round on Sempill. "*I* have not finished with you, Sempill, and you will not leave this house till you have told me what has become of the Spanish Letters."

"Then I fear I shall be your guest for longer than you would wish," Sempill retorted blandly. "You will never learn from me where they are."

The blood rushed darkly to Macey's face. He moved threateningly towards Sempill, but before he could reach him Marie had stretched out her hand in protest with a cry of:

"Wait! I can tell you where the letters are!"

"*What!*"

Macey's exclamation was echoed by them all. They closed round her in a tight expectant group, and looking up at the ring of tense faces she said calmly:

"They are in the charge of Sempill's manservant, Pringle, and he is on his way to Dover now to take ship with them for Spain."

15. Macey Rides South

To Jamie's surprise, and somewhat to his disappointment also, Macey did not take this revelation as an immediate signal to leap to horse and pursue Pringle. Instead, he began a careful cross-questioning of Marie that was later to develop into an even more careful planning of the line of action needed to deal with the situation.

First of all, however, he ordered Tod and Angus to take Sempill out of earshot. They marched him to the doorway end of the *salle d'armes* and his removal quietened the babble of talk round Marie and gave her a chance to speak.

"I would have told you about Pringle before this," she pointed out, "but at first I was too weak to talk and then you were all too concerned with Sempill to give me the opportunity! You see, Pringle was there with d'Aquirre and Sempill when I heard them talking, but it was not till after the quarrel over me that he was instructed what to do with the letters."

"What were the arrangements?" Macey asked. "Tell me as precisely as you can."

"D'Aquirre told him he was to follow Sempill down the tunnel to the lochside. Sempill would have a boat there waiting to take them to the far side of the loch and also, on the further bank, a horse ready saddled for the beginning of his journey. Thus he could leave the city without passing through any of the gates and so remain unobserved."

"You are *sure* Pringle was given the letters?"

"I will swear to it. D'Aquirre's very words to him were, '*His Majesty of Spain will greatly reward the bearer of this correspondence from his Scottish allies, so see to it that nothing prevents you from delivering the letters safely to him.'*"

Macey struck his fist into his palm in a sudden gesture of angry frustration. Between his teeth he said, "That is twice we have forgotten the existence of this fellow, Pringle — twice we have been lulled into ignoring him, and each time to our sorrow."

"There is no point in blaming yourself," the Cleek said consolingly. "You cannot be expected to remember everything."

Macey brushed the remark aside with fierce contempt. "How great a start does he have over me?" he demanded of Marie. "What time did he leave?"

"It was around midnight I think. I am not sure — it was difficult to keep account of time in that room."

"And what route was he told to follow?"

"I cannot tell you. They moved out of my hearing after the talk of the boat and I do not know what further was said."

Marie's voice slurred over the last few words and she began to tremble again with weakness and fatigue. Seeing this, Forbes held up his hand authoritatively, "Enough, Macey, she has told you all you need to know. Now she must rest."

Macey's expression changed from one of tense calculation to dismayed concern. He made as if to help Marie from her seat but Forbes forestalled him by swinging her light weight into his arms and striding from the room with her. They had a last glimpse of her face, pale, but still gallantly essaying a farewell smile as she looked back over her father's shoulder. Then she was gone and Macey returned to the problem of how to deal with Pringle.

"The fellow has a choice of three southward routes,"

he said to the Cleek. “He could travel the road that runs down the east coast — but that is the longest way and he will want to make as good time as possible. I think we can rule out the coast road. Now, the road over Soutra Hill is the shortest route of the three —”

“No one with any sense would ride Soutra at this time of the year,” the Cleek interrupted. “It is certain to be blocked by snow.”

“Then that leaves only the valley road by Galashiels and Jedburgh,” Macey decided.

He fell silent, deep in thought, and Jamie’s impatience for some kind of action to take the place of all this talk came to a head.

“Are you not going to ride the valley road after him, then?” he demanded, but Macey ignored this interruption to his line of thought. Turning to the Cleek he said:

“The problem here is not how to catch up with Pringle but how to outstrip him. If I ride, as I must, unaided, he could slip through my fingers. But if I can overhaul him without his knowledge then I can lay a trap ahead that is certain to catch him.”

He tapped the breast of his doublet in answer to the Cleek’s questioning look. “The Queen of England’s warrant lies safely hid here. Once over the border into my own country it will be all the power I need to summon a sufficient force to lie in wait and take him — at York I think would be the best place. Whichever road he rides he must pass through there eventually.”

The Cleek nodded. “Aye, all the roads south pass through York. But could you overhaul him in time to lay a trap there? He has nearly nine hours start of you if he left, as Mistress Marie thinks, around midnight last night.”

“Let me think,” Macey mused. “Edinburgh to

Galashiels, that is thirty miles. To Jedburgh is another sixteen or so."

"And rough going at that," the Cleek reminded him. "He would not dare push his mount at much more than a walking pace over that road in the hours of darkness."

"That means he would be no further than Galashiels by dawn this morning," Macey took up the thread, "and he would not consider that sufficient distance between himself and possible pursuit. But if he changed horses at Galashiels or Jedburgh he could ride on as far as Rochester by dusk today. Yes, I think he will sleep tonight at Rochester."

"And since he has almost certainly taken the valley route," the Cleek capped the argument, "you will be able to verify your reasoning on the way. That scarred face of Pringle's will make him easily remembered at any change house where he hires a fresh horse."

"Agreed, agreed! Now — say I could keep in the saddle long enough to pass him in Rochester tonight while he is asleep! I could then ride on past Rochester — to Riddesdale, perhaps. That would give me thirty miles start of him by tomorrow morning!"

The Cleek and he stared at one another, considering the feasibility of this project, and this time Jamie did not venture to interrupt their thoughts. The names of the towns they had mentioned meant nothing to him and never having journeyed further than Leith in his life he could only measure distance in terms of the length of a street. With the somewhat damping realization, therefore, that the conversation was completely over his head, he waited patiently for one of them to speak again, and eventually the Cleek said:

"Thirty miles is not much of a start for your purposes, Mr Macey."

Macey roused himself. “No, but I can increase on it. Look at it in this light. Pringle will be riding change house mounts from Rochester on — possibly even as early in the journey as Jedburgh, and if he wishes to continue hiring horses on the road south he will have to present each mount in good condition at every stage where he hopes to make a change. Therefore, fifty to sixty miles a day is the best he can hope for from a hired horse over winter roads in these circumstances. That means he can only cover from Rochester to Darlington tomorrow, and from Darlington to York on the following day. Three days riding in all — agreed?”

The Cleek nodded attentively and Macey continued, “Now, I can ride my own horse into the ground yet still, once I am over the border into England, use my warrant to enforce the hire of fresh horses. With this advantage I could make the journey in two stages — Edinburgh to Riddesdale today and Riddesdale to York tomorrow. Thus my thirty-mile lead at the end of the first day would be increased by another fifty miles. I would arrive in York a full day ahead of Pringle and this would give me ample time to lay my plans.”

The Cleek looked at him curiously. “Are you sure you realize the extent of the task you have set yourself?” he asked.

“I know very well,” Macey answered grimly, “but I know very well also that my country — and yours, will be at war if I fail. It must be done.”

The Cleek shrugged. “You had best be on your way then or time will be your master.”

Unexpectedly Macey flushed and in a somewhat flustered manner replied, “I must see Master Forbes before I go. Marie — er, that is, I have a matter of business to settle with him that will not await the outcome of the present affair.”

The Cleek cast a significant look to Jamie at this slip of the tongue on Macey's part, but there was not time to take it further for at that moment Forbes reappeared in the *salle d'armes*. He came briskly over to them and indicating Sempill still sullenly captive said in a low tone:

"This is a pretty problem we have on our hands now. What are we to do with him?"

"He is bound to guess that I will pursue Pringle," Macey said sharply, then dropping his voice, "We cannot loose him, Forbes. Why not turn him over to your authorities in Edinburgh?"

"I could not kill him in cold blood once I had heard Marie's story so how in honour can I let the Town Council do it for me?" Forbes protested. "There was sentence of death passed on him here in Edinburgh for his part in the Liège affair, I would have you remember, and that sentence is still in force."

"He could be kept here for a while," the Cleek suggested, but Forbes turned on him with a savage mutter of, "That is stretching tolerance too far! I will not house the man that murdered my brother — not even now that the debt is paid with Marie's life."

There was an uncomfortable silence during which Sempill's eyes travelled from one face to another. Clearly, although he was out of earshot, he was aware that his fate was under discussion and watching him Jamie wondered if he realized the impasse that confronted them.

Both Macey and Forbes were indebted to him for his efforts to prevent Marie's death, but Macey could not risk freeing him at this stage. Forbes would not house him, yet neither of them was prepared to take the cold-blooded decision to hand him over to the city hangman. He glanced at the Cleek wondering if the old man had any ingenious solution to the problem, but he looked as puzzled as the other two. It was like that time at the Anchor Inn, he thought, when the four of them had been faced by the same situation of deadlock caused by the capture of Marie.

It was the thought of Leith that brought a solution to the problem springing suddenly to Jamie's mind. "*The Northern Star!*" he thought triumphantly. It was one of the ships mentioned by the caddies who had kept watch on Leith docks, a brigantine due to sail in ballast to take on a cargo of timber at a Norwegian port. And her master, Captain Robertson, was a friend of Master Forbes!

He nudged the Cleek. "*The Northern Star!*" he whispered eagerly. "She is bound for Oslo on this afternoon's tide, remember? They could put him aboard her and turn him loose in Norway — 'twould at least keep him out of harm's way for a while."

The Cleek's exclamation at this turned into a crow of laughter that brought the eyes of Macey and Forbes sharply on them. "Tell them, Jamie," the Cleek chuckled. "Tell them this marvellous neat solution of yours!"

Diffidently Jamie explained his idea and when he had finished Forbes said thoughtfully, "Captain Robertson will certainly take him aboard if I ask him to and keep him close confined till he touches at Oslo." He turned to Macey, "What do you say?"

"We could not control his actions beyond the point of destination," Macey pointed out, and impatiently Forbes retorted, "At least in Norway and with a broken wrist to hamper him he could not prevent you catching Pringle. And that is the only matter of importance now."

It was the reminder of Pringle that spurred Macey's decision. "Very well," he agreed, "*The Northern Star* and a Norwegian destination let it be," and Forbes added with evident relief:

"Tod and Angus can escort him aboard between them."

Their voices had risen during the argument and the gist of what they were saying must have carried to Sempill for he waved his undamaged arm to them at this point, smiling and calling out something they did not catch. Ignoring him, Macey instructed:

"Make my horse ready for the road with all speed, Jamie. I shall join you at the stables in a few minutes."

As Jamie turned on his heel Macey took Forbes by the arm. "A word in your private ear, Forbes," he began quietly, but that was all Jamie heard before he was out of earshot and approaching the doorway of the *salle d'armes*.

Sempill's eyes were on him as he hurried to the door. He held himself erect again and with something like wonder Jamie noted that he had regained his former swaggering air. He smiled, his eyes twinkling merrily at Jamie as he approached.

"So I am not to be killed after all," he remarked.

Jamie nodded and would have passed on without comment but Sempill said quickly, "A moment, young sir. I have a question to ask."

Jamie paused in mid-step, fidgeting uneasily, not knowing whether or not he should listen, but Sempill gave him no time for doubts to gather into a decision.

"'Tis simply this," he hurried on. "Who was it that killed d'Aquirre?"

There was no harm in telling him that, Jamie decided, and briefly answered, "Mr Macey did," he was about to move on when Tod's deep voice added unexpectedly:

"It was Jamie here, all the same, that fought him

and held him at bay long enough for Macey to deal the stroke that killed him."

"I was caught in a position where I had to fight d'Aquirre in order to escape," Jamie amended Tod's version. "I was holding my own when I slipped and was knocked senseless by the fall. 'Twas at that moment that Macey came in and sprang to my rescue."

To his surprise and mortification then Sempill threw back his head and laughed, white teeth gleaming, red-gold beard quivering with merriment. Biting his lip he waited for the laughter to subside so that he could deliver the angry comment that was in his mind, but Sempill forestalled him. He cut off his laughter suddenly and looked smilingly down at Jamie.

"I have observed you," he said. "You are strong and bold and quick in the workings of your mind. And now I know also that you are lucky." His smile broadened. "You have all the attributes of an adventurer but that last is the most important of them all — luck!"

The word seemed to fascinate him for his hand descended on Jamie's shoulder and he repeated dreamily, "Luck, my boy — luck! 'Tis the most important gift of them all to those of our kind."

The uncomfortable feeling that he had already wasted too much time in talking made Jamie pull free of the hand on his shoulder and turn for the doorway, but before he was through it Sempill's voice rang out:

"Welcome, Jamie! Welcome to the ranks of the soldiers of fortune!"

Jamie glanced back and saw Sempill, white teeth gleaming again in the red-gold of his beard as he smiled broadly, his hand raised in mocking salute. Framed thus between his guards he made a lively picture that was in sharp contrast to his earlier dejection and instinctively Jamie's heart warmed to him. He waved and smiled in reply and ran out into the courtyard still smiling.

There was nothing ill-natured about Sempill he thought as he made for the stables. He was simply an adventurer, a man whose sword was for sale to the highest bidder. The words, "our kind" recurred to him, but with a shake of his head he rejected their meaning. He was not Sempill's kind. His sword could be for sale, yes, but not his loyalty to his country. But it was still possible to be a soldier of fortune in his country's cause — look at Macey! Was he not a soldier of fortune for England!

"*Welcome to the ranks of the soldiers of fortune!*" The gallant sound of the words rang a challenge in his mind all through the short time needed to check the harness of Macey's horse standing already saddled in the stable, and suddenly as he straightened up from tightening the girths, the idea the words had bred blossomed fully in his mind.

Quickly he moved over to the stall that housed a chestnut mare. She was a beautiful creature, high-bred and dainty-stepping with a turn of speed that he knew had won Master Forbes many a wager when he entered her for the races at Leith Links. "The perfect mount!" Jamie thought exultantly, heaving a saddle over the silky chestnut back. As for Master Forbes, surely he would account the loan of his chestnut mare a small thing in return for the rescue of his only daughter!

The chestnut saddled he led both horses out of the stable and began to rehearse a speech of explanation to Macey. It was ready on the tip of his tongue when Macey came hurrying across the courtyard but the surprise on his face at the sight of two horses sent all the fine words flying.

"I am coming with you, Mr Macey," he blurted out and turned to mount the chestnut mare.

Macey's exclamation of anger checked him with his foot still in the stirrup and he looked round in dismay.

"Unsaddle the mare," Macey told him curtly.

"But Mr Macey, I can ride," Jamie protested, "and I can use a sword. You may need me when it comes to the fighting."

Macey was in the saddle of the brown horse before he had finished speaking. He checked its forward plunge with a swift movement and leaned down to Jamie.

"Listen well," he said distinctly, "while I tell you how foolish you are. Firstly, when I fight this time it will be at the head of a troop of trained soldiers. I will have no need of a boy to flourish a romantic sword. Secondly, and most important, the city of York lies nearly two hundred miles from Edinburgh. Two hundred miles of mud and holes, of ruts and scattered stones. A fast rider with good changes of horse laid ready for him could cover it in three days — with luck! I will have to do it in two days."

His eyes bored into Jamie's. "Do you realize now what that means? It means I will have to ride this horse of mine till its brave heart bursts. Then I will have to do the same to another and yet another mount, but even though I leave a trail of broken and foundered horses in my wake, I will not be able to give in. I will have to stick in the saddle for two days and a night, never resting, never taking my eyes off the road, and at the end of that comes the planning and the fighting. You say you can ride, boy. Pah! You have not begun to learn the meaning of the word!"

The brutal directness of his speech stunned Jamie into silence, and realising possibly that he had achieved his aim with rather more force than was necessary, Macey added in a kindlier tone:

"It takes much training and many a hard year of soldiering to condition a man for such a task. Your spirit is equal to it, Jamie, I do not doubt, but you lack the training to accomplish it."

He shortened his grasp on the reins and touched knees to his mount. Jamie laid hold of the stirrup-leather and trotted by his side across the courtyard, a dull anger at Sempill for the falsely-bright vision he had inspired growing within him. Once more, as at the time of the discovery of the cypher, he was acutely aware of the gulf between himself and Macey. But this time it was not only in the field of learning. This time he could see clearly that the gulf was one of years of training and hardening, of stern discipline and self-sacrifice, and overwhelming his anger came a rush of embarrassment that he had aspired, even for a moment, to match his own petty abilities with those of such a man.

The feeling tied his tongue to such an extent that, as they reached the end of Beith's Wynd and turned into the High Street, he could only manage a muttered:

"Will you be returning to Edinburgh?"

"That I can promise you," Macey told him cheerfully. "I have unfinished business in Edinburgh that will bring me back here regardless of the outcome of this affair."

In spite of his own misery Jamie almost smiled at this. It was his courtship of Mistress Marie he was thinking about, of course — the slip of the tongue he and the Cleek had noted earlier had already made that plain — and no doubt the "private word" in Forbes's ear had concerned that also. Well, she was a bonnie lass and a brave one too, and Macey was a man after his own heart. They were well suited and he wished them good fortune, but …

With an effort to swallow the lump that disappointment had raised in his throat he gazed down at the toes of his worn shoes scuffing along the granite cobbles of the High Street, nodding assent as Macey warned:

"Do not relax your vigilance while I am gone, Jamie. Remember that Huntly and his associates are still free to strike. Take counsel with the Cleek and if danger to our cause threatens from that quarter you must do what you can to avert it. I will re-enter the city by the Netherbow Port when I do return. Do not fail to wait there for me."

He was gone before Jamie could think of a word to say in reply, and watching the erect figure on the brown horse trot smartly off down the High Street he was vividly reminded of that afternoon barely two weeks ago when Macey had come riding into his life. It had been cold then, he remembered, and he had shivered, glancing enviously at the warmth of the goldsmiths' booths. He was shivering now but not because of the east wind that blew so sharply up the High Street. The cold he felt now was inside him. It came from the sense of desolation that gripped him as horse and rider dwindled into the distance and disappeared from sight, and it was something that no fire could ever warm.

16. "Cock o' the North"

The wound in Jamie's shoulder healed very quickly. At the Cleek's request Nan put a proper dressing on it to replace Macey's makeshift one and this she changed carefully every day according to the procedure she had observed Marie to use in dressing wounds.

Each day when Nan had finished with him Jamie mounted to Marie's private parlour to enquire how she did. She also was mending rapidly and in a few days' time her accustomed health had returned. She was very cheerful and talked a great deal of Macey, not attempting to disguise her happiness in the prospect of marriage, but neither she nor her father made any further reference to her rescue from the de Guise palace.

This puzzled Jamie, for he had expected Forbes to be effusive in his thanks. However, thanks would only have embarrassed him in any case and he was content to let matters rest as they were.

He looked forward to his visits to the Forbes household but despite the fact that he was glad for Marie's happiness his own feeling of depression did not lessen, and as the days passed he began to understand the root cause of it. Always before, he realized, he had been content with his life as a caddie. It was a hard life but it was an independent one. It enabled him to speak his mind as he wished so that he was subservient to no man and it gave him the freedom of the city to use as he best liked.

There was no master to stop him when he had the fancy to visit the bear pits at Greenside or to spend an idle hour on Leith Links watching the golf and the archery or the horse racing. There was no stick waiting to be laid across his back for truancy if he decided to go for a swim in the Water of Leith or watch a hanging at the Tolbooth or try his courage at climbing the steep face of the rock on which the Castle perched high above the city.

There was no master in his life except hunger, no driving force except his own will. But neither was there any sense of purpose and this, he understood at last, was what the two weeks with Macey had given him. Moreover, it was a sense of purpose directed to a broader, fuller current of life than he had ever dreamed of, and for the first time in his life Edinburgh seemed to him to be a confining place in which to live. The city walls that had once spelt security to him suddenly seemed like the walls of a prison shutting him away from the world into which Macey had ridden — a world in which roads stretched for unthinkable distances to unknown cities and to far places where men proved themselves in battle.

Some of this he explained haltingly to Marie. "It will not always be so for you, Jamie, I promise," she said kindly. "Wait until M'sieu Macey returns and you will see."

They were back on to the subject of Macey's return, a subject dear to both their hearts and one that received fresh impetus on the day that his letter to Marie arrived from York. It was on the eighth day after his departure that Jamie mounted to her parlour to find both her and Forbes absorbed in the letter. Marie greeted him with a torrent of words from which he gathered that the letter had been sent off by special courier from York, four days before, and that it contained an account of Pringle's capture there.

"He is very thorough in his methods," Forbes said admiringly. "It seems that he had every change house in York surrounded by a guard of soldiery a full day before Pringle arrived there and the fellow rode straight into one of his traps."

"He is taking him with all haste to London to be interrogated by the English Privy Council," Marie added. "Pringle was carrying the Spanish Letters as I said he would be, so now the case against the conspirators is complete."

It should have been a matter for rejoicing, but somehow Jamie's spirits failed to rise to the occasion. If York was far away, he thought dismayed, how much further was the great city of London? It might take weeks for Macey to return from there!

"I — I thought Mr Macey would be coming straight back to Edinburgh," he said lamely, to cover his silence.

"Macey's duty lies in London," Forbes pointed out. "He cannot act on the evidence of the letters without further instructions from the English government — but he will come back to Edinburgh, never fear."

"But when?" Jamie asked. "How long does it take to ride from Edinburgh to London, Master Forbes?"

"The best time I have ever known it done in was a week," Forbes told him. "And that, mark you, was by an officer in my regiment who was a notable horseman."

"Then he *could* be back here in six days' time!" Jamie exclaimed. "Or seven, allowing for a day to accomplish his business in London."

Forbes laughed. "He would need to be a man of iron to leave Edinburgh on the twelfth day of the month and return again from London by the twenty-seventh! Besides, a body like the Privy Council will not make its decisions in a day. The wheels of government turn slowly, Jamie."

Marie looked up from her letter at this. "I do not

think he will have to wait long in London for his instructions," she said decisively. "The English Queen has been waiting for this evidence. She is shrewd, and she is frightened of the Spaniard. She will wish to strike quickly and hard. I think her Council will find it wise to decide very quickly what to do about the Spanish Letters."

It was the most comforting reflection that came of all their talk and speculation about Macey's letter, and one that Jamie came to rely on more and more in the days that followed its arrival. For it was only two days after this that the Earl of Huntly returned to Edinburgh.

Jamie was at the Netherbow Port at the time. He had been drawn there as by a magnet ever since the idea that Macey might return by the 27th had taken root in his mind. The Cleek was with him and Tod, who had been up at the west end of the High Street and so got wind of the Earl's entry through the West Port, came running down the High Street to tell them of his coming. The three caddies drew back into the shelter of the gate's great arch straddling the High Street and together they watched Huntly's progress towards them.

A mixed group of gentlemen and their servants rode behind him but they were all members of his own Highland clan of Gordon as could be seen from the plaids of dark green Gordon tartan they wore. The plaids apart, however, their dress fitted in well enough with the Lowland style of costume to attract little or no attention. It was the Earl himself who caught and held the eye.

He was mounted high on a tall black horse, a high-stepping mottled beast trapped out in silver, and adorned in the full regalia of a Highland chief. Instead of the green hunting Gordon tartan worn by the others he wore the dress tartan of his clan. Kilt and plaid were of vividly-checked blue and green and white and the plaid was caught at his shoulder with a silver pin set with the winking amber of a huge cairngorm jewel.

With one hand he held his mount's reins loosely gathered. The other hand rested lightly on the jewelled hilt of the short riding-sword by his side. His head was held at an arrogant tilt so that his black beard jutted out from the strong, hard line of his jaw. There was pride in every line of his appearance, from the delicate, high-stepping feet of the blood-horse that carried him to the chief's insignia of three eagle feathers flaring from his velvet bonnet, and as their eyes followed his passage through the Netherbow and into the Canongate the Cleek said meditatively:

"'Tis easy to see why it is they call him 'The Cock o' the North.'"

"Aye. They say he rules like a king himself up there in the northern parts," Tod agreed.

Jamie thought of Huntly's bold posture, the arrogant tilt of the dark head above the bright, glinting colours of his accoutrements and with a smile he remarked, "The name suits him. He is bold enough and finely feathered."

Tod laughed but the Cleek said soberly, "Save your wit, Jamie. Huntly looked as pleased with himself as a cat that has just lapped a dish of cream and, mark my words, that means he has some mischief planned."

The Cleek's pessimism was soon fully justified. No great body of clansmen that would have alarmed the citizentry followed the Earl into the city. Instead, they came in a steady trickle, entering by the various gates in small groups and avoiding Huntly House to take up residence in the many small hostelries in the city. The dark green of the Gordon tartan became a commonplace sight in the course of the next few days, but despite the fact that the Huntly men remained quiet and unobtrusive in their behaviour a feeling of tension began to gather over the city.

Jamie caught it in the furtive looks people cast over their shoulders, in sudden pauses in conversation, in the indefinable air the city had of waiting for something to happen.

"What do you think Huntly has in mind to do, Cleek?" he asked uneasily. "It was not part of his plan to capture the city till he had linked up with the Spaniard, yet he has enough men here to do that now. Do you think that is his aim?"

The Cleek sighed. "Who can tell? Huntly is a rash man and very proud. It could well be that he means to anticipate the main plan — perhaps with the thought that a single-handed success would gain him more honour in the Spanish king's eye."

It was early in the morning of the 27th of February that their conversation took place and Huntly's men had been infiltrating into the city for five days, during which Jamie had kept constant watch at the Netherbow Port. They were standing there now, the Cleek huddled back into the shelter of the arch and Jamie restlessly pacing back and forth with his head constantly turning to look down the Canongate. This was the day he had fixed on as the earliest possible date for Macey's return and his mind was filled with alternate hope and dread as he talked — hope that Macey would appear miraculously to take charge of the situation, and dread of Huntly's mysterious plans.

"What *is* Huntly planning to do?" he wondered aloud.

"Oh, hold your tongue, boy," the Cleek snapped. "I know no more than you do."

The impatient tone was a measure of his concern for the Cleek's self-assurance seldom failed him. There was several minutes' silence after this exchange then the clock on the Canongate church struck eight and the Cleek moved out of the shadow of the arch.

"The king rides forth from Holyrood to the Tolbooth today to sit in session with the Lords and Justices," he said. "Look there."

He pointed towards Holyrood House, and following the pointing finger Jamie saw a quick flash of colour and glinting metal. A few minutes later the first of the heralds and outriders in the royal procession appeared at the foot of the Canongate, the sun gleaming on the red and gold of their tabards and striking points of light from the metal of their mounts' harness. A cavalcade of nobility that filled the whole breadth of the Canongate came on behind the heralds. A trumpet rang out, pennants fluttered, a clatter of hooves, voices, the sound of laughter filled the clear morning air. Then the long slender shaft that bore the royal ensign appeared rising proudly up from the centre of the procession.

Quickly Jamie leapt on to a mounting-block beside the gate, and from this vantage point as the procession passed him saw, first the herald who bore the ensign and then the king himself. He was smiling and talking as he rode, a pale young man, red-bearded and a little inclined to stoutness, not gorgeously dressed as were the noblemen surrounding him, and with no great presence about him although he sat his horse well.

All this Jamie noted in a flash, and in the same instant of heightened perception he saw also the cat-like glint of triumph in Huntly's eyes as he bent to exchange words with the king, saw Bothwell, broad-shouldered and impassive riding behind the two of them, and identified the faces of the other conspirators in the mounted throng.

They swept past him, brilliant in silk and silver, velvet and gold, the greatest assemblage of wealth and power that Scotland had to show. There were men there who carried a fortune in jewels on their fingers, and men on whose faces power and ambition for power was openly written. And yet, Jamie thought wonderingly as he watched them disappear up the High Street, it was still the pale young man in the rather shabby doublet who had impressed him. There was something about him that set him apart from the others, an indefinable air, a look —

Still groping for the words that would express his feelings he heard the Cleek at his elbow saying, "I fear me for the king's life, Jamie," and sliding down from the block saw to his dismay that there were actually tears standing in the old man's eyes.

A cold shiver ran over him at the sight of the mournful face and the ominous ring of the words. "Huntly did not plan to kill the king," he protested. "It was only intended to take him captive."

"Kings have a way of dying in captivity," the old man said bitterly. "I would not give a bent bawbee for James Stewart's life if he fell into Spanish hands!"

"They would not dare!" Jamie muttered, but his words carried no conviction even to himself. He glanced up and down the High Street remembering all the armed and furtive Huntly men skulking in taverns and mingling unobtrusively with the citizens. Where were they now? Were they gathering round the Tolbooth, surrounding it so that the king would be trapped once he had entered there?

It was something that could easily be done, he thought, remembering the odd position the building occupied. It stood a short way up from the Market Cross and had been built, for some reason that he had never learned, right in the middle of the roadway, so that it split the High Street into two narrow alleys running one on either side of it. Like an island it stood in the dry river of the roadway. There would be nothing easier than to surround it!

"I am going off to the Tolbooth," the Cleek said suddenly. "Will you come?"

Jamie shook his head and the old man shrugged. "Keep your watch if you must," he said wearily, "but I doubt you will be disappointed."

He hobbled away, a bent but still grimly determined old man, and Jamie was left to his interminable watching of the Canongate. The morning's traffic through the Netherbow built up to a steady flow. Carts squeaked through with cargoes off-loaded at Leith. A party of ladies with hawks on their wrists rode by in a swish of silks and a high flutter of voices. A fish-wife screamed protest at the gatekeeper for the toll he charged on the creel of herring she had brought to sell in the city. Merchants and market wives pushed past him. The town herdsman drove a squealing horde of pigs through the gate. Everything was as usual as the morning dragged by.

At ten o'clock the Cleek returned with Tod and ten or so other caddies. "Huntly's men are all round the Tolbooth," he told Jamie grimly. "There is no display of arms as yet but I doubt the king will not return to Holyrood today."

It was a shock to hear what had been only fears and doubts thus transformed to an actual threat and Jamie stared at him in dismay.

"You truly think Huntly means to take the king prisoner?"

The Cleek picked his words with care. "I think there is real danger that such is his purpose."

Tod asked, "How long will it be before he moves openly against the king, Cleek?"

"The king rises for dinner at twelve noon," the Cleek told him. "I think Huntly has timed it for then. The whole city will be sitting down to meat and the streets will be clear."

More caddies came hurrying down the High Street towards the Netherbow. They were talking excitedly among themselves but they quietened down as they reached the gate.

"What's to do then, Cleek?" several voices asked.

"Nothing, yet," the old man said curtly. "If we act before Huntly strikes it will only recoil on our own heads for he will deny his purpose and the king will believe him."

"Macey could convince the king," Jamie said, but his eyes were on the clock and he spoke without hope for the hands stood now at half-past ten. To his surprise, however, the Cleek snatched at his words. "Aye, he has the evidence," he agreed. "'Tis a slim hope that he will arrive in time to use it but 'tis all we have for the moment. We must wait here meantime."

Silence fell on the group of caddies. They numbered around fifty now so that they partly blocked the gate and many a curious glance and angry shout was thrown at them. The caddies ignored them all. They stood or squatted in groups around the gate, all eyes turned to the church clock. The minute hand swept slowly up to eleven o'clock and began its slow dive down towards the half-hour. Several times a lone rider came towards them up the Canongate but none of them was the tall man on the brown horse that Jamie looked for so eagerly.

The minute hand touched the half-hour. It crept onwards for another five minutes. A restless stir broke out among the caddies. The long black pointer jerked forward another minute on the dial and the whispering voices rose to an angry murmur. The Cleek stepped forward and raised his arms for silence.

"Gather round, lads," he shouted. "Here is what you have to do."

17. The March of the Caddies

Jamie did not move from his position as the caddies crowded round the Cleek. There was a rider coming up the Canongate but his horse was not brown, it was dapple-grey, and the man himself was not tall in the saddle. Still Jamie waited, hope warring faintly with despair in his heart. The rider came on at a fast trot and instinctively Jamie winced to see the spurs rowel deep into the grey's flanks and blood run thinly down its dappled hide.

The rider raised his head bent low over the flowing mane. He was a dozen yards away, his face was streaked with mud and twisted with fatigue, but even so he was recognisable. Jamie's heart gave a great twist of excitement in his chest. He choked, his breath rising in a great bubble of sound in his throat.

"*Macey!*" he shrieked. "*Cleek, it's Macey!*"

He had no clear memory of what was said or done in the few seconds that followed. The next thing he knew he was clinging to the grey's stirrup-leather and Macey was looking down on him from blood-shot eyes and asking hoarsely:

"The king — where will I find the king?"

"At the Tolbooth," he gasped and was almost thrown aside as Macey spurred the grey again. He hung on desperately and the rest of the caddies closed in blocking Macey's path. "Wait! Huntly is with him!" Jamie shouted, but his voice was lost in the din.

The Cleek clove a way to the front of the throng, angrily laying about him with his golf club. His voice rose above the others, explaining the situation, and Macey's tired face grew fierce with anger.

"I have the letters on me, Cleek," he said crisply, "also a dispatch from Queen Elizabeth writ with her own hand and imploring the king to put Huntly under lock and key or else take the consequences of her wrath. That will convince King James. Now let me pass."

"But if Huntly gets the least inkling of what is in that dispatch he will still strike!" the Cleek cried. "We must still rouse the city as I meant to do before you came."

"A mob to combat armed and trained fighting-men?" Macey asked sceptically.

A low growl ran round the ranks of the caddies. "Have you ever seen an Edinburgh mob rioting in defence of a Stewart king?" the Cleek asked derisively. "They will tear Huntly's men limb from limb!"

The words and a repeated growl of anger from the caddies convinced Macey. "Can you do it in the time that is left?" he asked.

"We have fifteen minutes," the Cleek told him. "That is enough."

"Clear the way!" he shouted to the caddies. They fell back. The grey plunged forward and Macey was off up the High Street. Tod grabbed Jamie's shoulder and started him off in the same direction.

"The fleetest of us are to run to the west end and rouse the citizens there," he explained as they ran. "We will join up at the Tolbooth with those coming from the east end of the street."

Other caddies were running shoulder to shoulder with them. "The cry is '*Treason,*'" a voice panted in Jamie's ear. He nodded, saving his breath for the fast pace Tod's long legs were setting. Macey had drawn well ahead, his progress clearing a way for them through the crowded street and as they reached

Geddies Close just short of the Market Cross he disappeared from view.

Their group split at this point, half of it bearing north from the High Street, the other half bearing south. Jamie and Tod were in the north-bound sector and they poured into Geddies Close in a rush of voices and pounding feet.

"*All out! All out! All out!*"

Jamie's voice soared with the rest, reverberating from the fronts of the tall houses lining the narrow alley. All down its length shutters flew wide and heads peered down at the caddies' hands cupped round mouths, arms frenziedly beckoning.

"*Treason!*" Jamie yelled. "*All out to the Tolbooth! Treas-o-o-on!*"

From Geddies Close to Anchor Close, on to Craig Close and Roxburghe Close the warning shouts rang out, echoing and reverberating down the deep narrow canyons of the houses. Scattered now from the main group, each caddie bore his separate spearhead of alarm towards the head of the High Street. Their voices carried to Jamie beating his way west up Shank's Close beyond the Tolbooth and sudden inspiration seized him as he passed under the sign of a barrel hung outside the shop of John Greaves, a cooper.

Greaves, this year, was the custodian of the Blue Blanket, the banner of the trades!

A blow from his fist sent the door of Greaves's shop crashing back on its hinges. Inside, the cooper and his two apprentices jerked to startled attention at the apparition — hair wild, cheeks scarlet with exertion, that appeared in the doorway.

"*Treason!* Jamie bellowed into their astonished faces. "*Rally to the Tolbooth! The king is betrayed!*"

The cooper's hammer fell from his hands. His voice

shouting, "*Up with the Blue Blanket!*" followed Jamie out into the street but he did not stay to see the famous signal hoisted. On through Blythe's, Todd's, and Nairn's Closes he sped, his lungs labouring now and voice hoarse but still loud and urgent enough to bring heads to the windows and bodies tumbling in panic of alarm into the streets. Rounding the corner into Bell's Close he crashed into Tod. Breathless, they hung on to one another.

Sound swelled all around them. Shouts, shrieks, commands, echoed among the houses. And from every direction came the sound of feet — feet pattering, tramping, running, a great beat and clatter of feet that brought their glances together in a grin of mutual triumph.

Tod now had a cudgel in his hand, a great knotted stave of wood. He flourished it above his head, narrowly missing a stout market wife running past him with a poker ferociously upraised.

"*To the Tolbooth!*" His voice boomed out like a great bass bell. The gathering crowd in Bell's Close fell in behind him. Jamie drew his sword and pounded along beside Tod, out into the High Street. Tod's great weight drove a passage through to the forefront of the gathering mob. Caddies came darting from left and right, from Kennedy's Close and Ross's Close. They were armed. Suddenly, miraculously, everyone was armed.

Cleavers, axes, pitchforks, knives, swords, hammers, flashed and gleamed. The mob, like a many-fanged monster, clashed its misshapen teeth in hungry anticipation of blood. A sound that was part roar part howl rose from its hundreds of throats, and from the east end of the High Street came a long-drawn-out answering howl.

They surged forward, Jamie and the caddies in line abreast leading at a half-run down the street. The Blue Blanket dipped and fluttered in their midst its folds spreading over the tools of trade turned to weapons of war, but for once, Jamie thought exultantly, the craftsmen were being led by the craftless, the disinherited, the caddies.

The Tolbooth loomed, a black, ungainly pile as grim as the justice that was dealt within its walls. Outside it surged a wild mêleé of kicking, screaming horses. The caddies left in charge of the horses of those inside were goading and turning them loose among the besiegers of the building. The solid block of green-tartaned men broke to let the horses through then closed ranks again. Huntly's men were standing firm.

But not for long. "*Not for long!*" Jamie yelled the challenge aloud as the mob closed with the ranks of the traitors. The mob's own spirit of savage recklessness filled him, trickling over his tongue like the hot, fiery taste of strong wine, rising to his brain in fumes that blurred reason and blunted the sense of danger.

He struck out furiously at a stocky Highlander swinging the broad blade of a claymore at his head. The blow would have sent his head rolling on the cobbles if a brawny arm wielding a hammer had not deflected the Highlander's stroke. He staggered, gasping, and the claymore whistled harmlessly past Jamie's cheek as he lunged. The Highlander fell to his stroke but he had barely time to disengage before he was caught and swung round to face a dirk travelling hard for his throat. He feinted, ducked, and brought his left elbow driving vigorously into the attacker's windpipe. A foot hooked round his right leg. He was dragged off balance and staggered forward, fending off in his blundering course, the stroke of a claymore that would have pierced a woman armed with a poker.

It was the same woman who had run so determinedly past him in Bell's Close. Other faces now, he recognized. The Cleek, like an ancient, avenging demon, cracking skulls with his golf club with the careless skill of a woman cracking eggs. Cuddy and Daddler, the inseparable pair, fighting back to back each with a pair of horse's brasses wrapped round his knuckles. Lucky Finlayson, ungainly and ponderous with his one-legged stance but still swinging his cherished old sword in orthodox military style. And Tod, the gentle giant, transformed now into a roaring berserk colossus — a Crusader leapt to life from the tombs of Saint Giles, Tod the knight-errant of the streets with only a club in his hand for weapon but the true fire of justice in his soul.

Other faces he saw while the battle ebbed and flowed round him and his sword wove a steel circle of safety against the weapons that flashed at him from every side, all faces that he knew, some well some only in the passing: the faces of tradesmen, and merchants, 'prentices and market-women, water-carriers and chimney sweeps. For now the faces of the Edinburgh folk were out-numbering the driven desperate faces of the Huntly men. The mob was in the ascendant. The green tartan was broken and scattered over the breadth of the High Street, fleeing solitary to be cut down by howling pursuit, backed up in groups in last-ditch defiance against the house walls. The mob had won.

"We have won, boy — put up your sword!"

It was the Cleek, his hand tugging at Jamie's shoulder, his voice cracked and trembling with excitement. He began to say something in reply but to his surprise found that his own voice was trembling just as badly and contented himself with a nod and a smile. Taking deep breaths to bring his voice under control again he turned to the Tolbooth and saw the door swinging open.

There was a glint of red from the shadows within and suddenly the king appeared at the head of the steps leading up to the doorway. With one hand he was leaning on Macey's shoulder and with the other he clasped a sheaf of papers. He was pale, his hair dishevelled, like a man in the throes of shock, but when the roar of the crowd swelled out to him he took his hand from Macey's shoulder and raised it commandingly.

"Good people!" he cried. "We love you for your loyalty! But for the rest, We are betrayed, most shamefully betrayed by one that should have loved Us. Behold the traitor!"

Macey stood aside. Two men filled his place, the Earl of Huntly and the Captain of the Castle Guard. Huntly's face was red with anger and his lips were tightly compressed. He did not blink or alter countenance at the yell of execration that greeted him. Once again the king quietened the crowd.

"See that he is brought safely to Holyrood," he called warningly. "Do not let your anger anticipate Our justice!"

He moved forward down the steps. The crowd surged joyfully to meet him, caught him up, and raised him shoulder-high. Jamie was borne with them, smothered and crushed by the impact of the massed bodies. He surfaced, bruised and gasping, and looking dazedly around saw the figure of the king still carried shoulder-high being borne eastward down the street towards Holyrood.

The Captain of the Guard was descending the steps

with Huntly and the remnants of the crowd closed round them, hooting and jeering. As prisoner and escort moved off, Jamie glimpsed Macey struggling to reach them. He was impatiently cuffing heads and shouldering aside the people who impeded his path and suddenly Jamie felt laughter welling up to release the tension inside him. He fought his way to Macey's side and still laughing, gasped out:

"You would not be so free with your hands if you had seen this mob a few minutes ago!"

Macey grasped his arm. "The time is not yet for mirth," he snapped. "Not till Huntly is under lock and key!"

He forged ahead and Jamie pressed closely behind him, all laughter forgotten. In front of them the plumes on the helmet of the Captain of the Guard bobbed above the heads of the crowd. They were still jeering as they moved along beside Huntly and his escort but they were no longer the tight-packed mob that had closed round him at the foot of the steps. They opened easily to let Macey buffet his way to the front and within a few minutes he and Jamie had drawn level with the prisoner.

Huntly saw them. His eyes slid side-long in a venomous glance at Macey, but he did not break step. He looked ahead again and it occurred to Jamie that he was remarkably self-possessed for a man in his position. He shot a puzzled look at Macey and received a warning frown that told him to keep his eyes on Huntly. Macey himself was striding along alert as a hunting cat. Not once in the long progress down the High Street did he take his eyes off the prisoner, but neither did Huntly's composure crack.

He was too composed, Jamie decided as they passed through the Netherbow. He glanced towards Huntly

House coming up on their right and his hand closed round the hilt of his sword. They drew level with the arch that spanned the entrance to the courtyard at the side of the house and with breath-taking suddenness Huntly exploded into action. A sideways leap took him into the shadow of the arch. Quicker than a cat turning he was on to the back of the saddled horse that waited there and plunging through the shouting guards.

Jamie had leapt after him with the others. Now he saw his mistake as the iron-shod hooves struck out among them in that confined space. He backed against the wall and from the corner of his eye saw the horse plunge into the street. In the same moment Macey's flying form crossed his view as he leapt to straddle the horse behind Huntly.

His right arm came up catching the Earl under the chin. Huntly's head was forced back. His hands dropped from the reins and the terrified horse reared wildly. Macey and Huntly crashed together to the cobbles in a writhing, struggling heap and Huntly's escape bid was over. The guard was on him and the Captain, his face livid with anger, gave the command to bind his hands.

Too angry even to thank Macey he set his procession in motion again, and this time the point of his sword was pressed against Huntly's back as they marched the remaining short distance to Holyrood. Jamie made a move to follow them, but Macey's out-stretched hand stopped him.

"The captain is well warned. It will not happen again," he said quietly. "You and I have done our share, Jamie."

Jamie turned to look at him. "It has all happened so quickly since you came back," he said. "I can hardly believe it is all over."

Macey looked up smiling from brushing the mud off his clothes. "It is not all over yet," he said gaily. "I still have unfinished business at Master Forbes's house, you will recall. And that is where we are going now."

18. A New Horizon

The wedding of Marie Forbes to Roger Macey took place at ten o'clock in the morning two days after Huntly's examination by the king at Holyrood and committal to the Castle on a charge of high treason.

Marie having expressed the desire to be married from her father's house and the *salle d'armes* being the largest room in which guests could be accommodated, it was suitably decorated in the interim and the ceremony took place there. The guests included some notable figures, Forbes himself being a person of some consequence in the city, but the most distinguished of these was Sir Robert Bowes, the English Ambassador, who had attended as a mark of Queen Elizabeth's special favour to Macey. A further and much more impressive token of her esteem emerged as the climax to Macey's account of his reception in London with Pringle as his prisoner — a tale which emerged gradually in detail after the first hurried account he had given them on the day of Huntly's arrest.

"You have heard the expression, 'a right royal rage,'" he began his story of the meeting of the English Privy Council, "but I will wager none of you have seen it so admirably applied as I did that day. The translation of the correspondence with the Spaniard took only a few hours once I had handed over the key of the cypher to Lord Burghley, the English Chancellor. He set his clerks to copy the letters in a plain version while Pringle was being interrogated and Queen Elizabeth had them ready in her hand when she swept into the Council chamber.

"She has long white hands, you must know, very delicate-looking hands of which she is exceeding vain, and her voice in normal speech is inclined to a high and somewhat mincing tone. But when she is angry she doubles her hands into fists as a man would do and her voice comes out deep and roaring — the very voice, I am told, of her father King Harry.

"Like this then, she harangued the English Council. She struck her fists against the table and swore with oaths such as a man would use that no Prince (meaning King James), should nourish such traitorous rogues in his kingdom or he were not a true Prince. But she, Elizabeth, would uphold the honour of Princes, and that right hastily. Then she called for pen and ink and with her own hand she wrote a dispatch to King James bidding him, '*as he loved her and her kingdom to clap the traitors up in gaol forthwith —*.'"

"But surely," Jamie interrupted, "the English queen cannot bid our king to do her will as she pleases? How could she know he would obey?"

Macey and Forbes exchanged smiles over his head and Forbes said, "You are in the realm of high politics now, Jamie. King James is the nearest relation in blood the English queen has and he will in due time succeed to her throne. But, '*as he loved her and her kingdom*' was a very strong threat that she might will the English crown away from him to another claimant if he offended her."

"So you see, you and I will have the same Sovereign at some future date," Macey said. "Remember that when a future decision faces you, Jamie."

And without giving Jamie an opportunity to query this rather cryptic remark he went on:

"The letter signed and sealed, she stood up and called me to her. I knelt to receive her commands and she said, 'Lend me your sword, Lord Burghley.' Then, while I was still pondering what use she had for a sword at that moment I felt it lightly touch one shoulder and then the other and I heard Queen Elizabeth's voice saying, "Rise, *Sir* Roger Macey."'"

A shout of delight ran round his listeners and everyone crowded round to shake his hand. Forbes, with a guffaw of laughter pinched Marie's ear and teased her, "So you are to be a *Lady* Macey, eh!" And Marie, blushing, received her share of the congratulations.

When they were quiet again, Macey went on with his story. "I had hardly got my breath back after this surprise," he said, "when the Queen asked me to ride forthwith to Edinburgh again and seek out immediate audience with King James."

Marie and Jamie exchanged looks and Forbes said, grinning, "These two were sure you would scarce be given time to turn round in London and they held fast to their theory in the face of all argument to the contrary."

Macey smiled wryly. "Then they knew Queen Elizabeth better than I thought I did! I was so weary I could scarce stand on my feet, but said she, 'This affair must be carried quickly to a conclusion and you are the man best fitted to do so.' And so, mud and travel-stained and weary as I was, I took horse again that day for Edinburgh."

He looked round them all, spreading out his hands in a gesture of wonder. "Heaven was with me," he said soberly, "or I could not have survived the fatigue of that second journey or completed it in time to arrive when I did."

"Heaven was undoubtedly on your side," Forbes agreed, "but you have your own hardihood to thank for the greater part of it. I said before and I say it again now that only a man of iron could carry out such a feat of endurance, and I am proud that my daughter should marry you."

It was a sentiment that was echoed on every hand. King James himself — his grief over Huntly's betrayal somewhat comforted by the unexpected ownership of the Spanish gold, set the seal of his approval on the marriage by bestowing a fine necklace of pearls on Marie as a wedding gift. These he presented to Macey following his attendance to give evidence at Huntly's examination — a proceeding which, together with the purchase of more suitable clothes than his travel-stained garments, took up most of Macey's time before the wedding.

Jamie, with no money to buy clothes but two days' time in which to make himself fit to be seen in the wedding company, had to be content with Nan's washing and careful mending of his old garments. Tod took him in hand after this and cropped his untidy shock of hair into a semblance of elegance and with Norton's blue cloak draped over his shoulder he thought he looked presentable enough. The Cleek, however, who had dressed for the occasion in a doublet of red velvet inherited from Master George Heriot the jeweller and who looked in his shabby finery like a demon king fallen on hard times, had a different verdict on Jamie's efforts. Surveying him with a mixture of curiosity and approval he remarked:

"You look older, Jamie. If I did not know that you are still a reckless, headstrong boy at heart I would say that the last month had made a man out of you."

Jamie took both the compliment and the sting in its tail with equal grace. The Cleek's tongue had always been sharp, he thought tolerantly, and when they walked into the long hall where the wedding company was gathered he glanced affectionately from the old man hobbling on one side of him to Tod, big and neat and quiet as ever, on the other. Never again, he knew, would he have such true friends, and knew too that however distasteful the life of a caddie had grown to him it would never be completely unbearable while he had Tod and the Cleek beside him.

They took their places unobtrusively and murmured in admiration along with the rest as Marie entered on her father's arm. She was very lovely in her wedding dress of blue taffeta silk with a film of delicate white lace on her dark hair and King James's pearls gleaming at her throat. She walked slowly, one hand lying lightly on her father's arm, so ethereal in her cloud of lace and shimmering silk that she seemed like a creature from another world. But when she drew level with the three caddies she glanced aside and her normal, everyday self peeped briefly out in the smile that gleamed in her eyes and trembled momentarily round her mouth.

Jamie smiled in return, his thoughts racing back to the moment of decision before he entered the secret tunnel. He had been right then, he thought, and he was right now. This was no fragile doll, no delicate miss, or aery-faery creature of finer clay than others. There was a brave, hard core of steel in Marie Forbes. She had the courage needed in the wife of a man who lived as dangerously as Macey.

The murmured words of the ceremony were soon over and in no time at all, it seemed, Marie had tossed her bouquet of flowers as a signal for the dancing to begin and Macey had presented the Cleek with a wedding purse to use, "as he thought fit." It was an unusually heavy wedding purse as the Cleek pointed out when he displayed it gleefully to Tod and Jamie. The caddies would be well compensated for their efforts on Macey's behalf.

The fiddles and viols had been shrilling out for an hour before Marie and Macey left the *salle d'armes* to change into travelling clothes for their journey south. They slipped out unobtrusively, apparently with the intention of avoiding a going-away ceremony with its attendant pranks played by the guests, and with their going Jamie's light-heartedness vanished.

When the reel he was dancing in ended he left the *salle d'armes* and walked quickly through the long outer passage to the front door. At least, he thought, he could watch unseen as Macey left Edinburgh for good. And hoped as he walked that he was man enough now to swallow the bitterness of that pill without repining.

In the shadow of the doorway he paused and watched the group gathered by the three horses, two saddled and the third loaded as a baggage animal. There was only Sir Robert Bowes and Forbes himself taking farewell of Marie and Macey, and the Ambassador was the first to leave the group.

He came striding towards Jamie, a tall, spare figure, very elegant in black velvet with a glittering diamond Order on his chest, and passing him by without a glance he re-entered the house. Jamie made a wry face behind his back. Would the Ambassador have been so haughty, he wondered ruefully, if he had known how large a part the shabby boy in the doorway had played in the recovery of the Spanish Letters?

Forbes turned in his direction then and waved a beckoning arm, and with a flush of embarrassment at being thus discovered lingering uninvited near the scene of farewell, Jamie walked forward. Forbes's greeting, however, showed that he thought very differently of Jamie's presence.

"We have been waiting till your dance was finished before I came to fetch you," he said, "but now that you have found your way —"

He gestured towards Macey who turned from helping Marie to mount. She took the reins into her hands and smiled down at Jamie and Macey said:

"Jamie, I have received the impression that you have an inclination to pursue the kind of work that I am engaged in, and you seem also to me to be the kind of lad that is well suited to it. I have a proposal to put to you if you care to listen."

Jamie nodded, unable to find any words to express the wild surmises that were rushing through his brain. Macey looked from him to Forbes and went on:

"You may have found it strange that Master Forbes expressed none of his feelings of gratitude for the part you played in Lady Macey's rescue from d'Aquirre, but this was because he knew of the proposal I have for you and did not wish to anticipate it. Briefly, it is this. We both owe you a debt that cannot be repaid in thanks or money but possibly may be met by granting you your heart's desire. Therefore, Master Forbes has agreed to keep you at our joint expense for a period of up to two years, in which time you will be thoroughly tutored in sword-play of all kinds and in all the allied arts of defence. You will also receive such schooling as will enable you to proceed to the study of maps and cyphers such as are used in my kind of employment once you have joined me in England."

He paused and looked searchingly at Jamie. "That is, if you wish to join me. You will recall how I reminded you that your king would one day rule over both our countries and it should not offend your conscience therefore if I say that I can safely offer you a position in the Service to which I belong."

"I—I —" Jamie stuttered.

"He says 'Yes,'" Marie said decisively. She laughed down at him. "You *do* say 'yes,' Jamie?"

"Yes, yes, yes! With all my heart, yes!" Jamie's voice suddenly released from its bondage fairly rattled the words out in a great shout of acquiescence. Marie extended her hand to him.

"I am very pleased, Jamie Morton," she said quietly. "I owe you my life and I shall never forget that."

The words and the way she looked at him told Jamie that she too had had a hand in this offer and he recalled her promise, so lightly received at the time, that all would be different for him when Macey returned.

"Your servant, Lady Marie, your loyal servant!" he said fervently, and bent to kiss the hand she held out to him.

"'Tis not goodbye, Jamie," Macey said cheerfully. "Only, 'till we meet again,' and the harder your efforts of study are the sooner that day will be."

A firm hand-clasp and he was in the saddle. Marie bent for a last embrace from her father, Forbes and Macey clasped hands, then the two of them were riding quickly off towards the High Street. Forbes followed slowly with Jamie by his side and at the end of Beith's Wynd they stopped, watching and waving as the two figures disappeared down the High Street. Forbes turned a melancholy face towards Jamie and sighing deeply laid a hand on his shoulder.

In silence they walked like this back to the house, each sunk in his own thoughts. For Jamie, the glorious prospect before him was still blurred by the inevitable ache of parting, and what Forbes's feelings were at losing his beloved only daughter, he could only guess at. He would have liked to tender his sympathy but out of respect for the fencing master's disinclination to talk he remained silent till they entered the house. Only then, as they walked down the passage past Forbes's study to the *salle d'armes*, he said hesitantly:

"I am very grateful, Master Forbes, for the opportunity you offer me. I shall do my best to prove an apt pupil."

Forbes halted his stride. He looked closely at Jamie in the dim light of the passage then suddenly he flung open the study door and drew Jamie inside with him. He lifted a pair of foils from their case on his desk and turning to Jamie said briskly:

"A truce to sadness and all this mawkish talk of gratitude! Your part in the affair of the Spanish Letters has earned you a new life, Jamie. When would you like to begin it?"

Jamie looked longingly at the twin shafts of steel gleaming in the fencing master's hands.

"Now!" he said firmly. "This very moment."

"Now let it be," Forbes agreed. He handed Jamie a blade. "On your mark, Morton."

They took up position, blades raised in salute, and Forbes called, "*En garde!*"

They lunged, their blades crossed, and a tingle ran up Jamie's arm — a tingle that was not only the vibration of the steel but which he felt then as a thrill of pure joy.

Forbes caught the infection of his pleasure and his bearded face split in a huge grin over the crossed blades. Canny Scotsman as he was, however, he disengaged with the warning:

"Easy, Jamie. You have a lot to learn yet before you take London by storm."

"Then teach me!" Jamie cried. "For I mean to do so, and that right soon!"

Once again he closed with Forbes, and this time the lesson began in earnest.

The Thirteenth Member

Mollie Hunter

On a dark night in the 1590s Adam has a terrifying glimpse of the Devil. He is even more alarmed when he discovers that Gilly, the kitchen maid, is the thirteenth member of a witches' coven.

Adam is determined to foil the coven's plot to kill Scotland's king. But can he save Gilly?

Kelpies

A Pistol in Greenyards

Mollie Hunter

In 1854 the tenants of Greenyards, in the Scottish Highlands, are brutally evicted from their homes and the land sold for sheep grazing.

To defend his family Connal Ross draws a pistol on the local Sheriff-Officer ... a crime punishable by death. Will Connal and his sister, Katrine ever be able to start a new life, and escape to freedom?

Kelpies

A Stranger Came Ashore

Mollie Hunter

When a young man literally stumbles out of a stormy sea into the islanders' lives, few sense something uncanny about him. Handsome and charming he steals everyone's hearts. Yet Robbie, haunted by tales of the Selkie folk, is inexplicably disturbed by him. And when everything falls into place, it seems that no one has the power to help Robbie ...

Kelpies

Escape From Loch Leven

Mollie Hunter

Mary, Queen of Scots, is imprisoned at Loch Leven Castle, enchanting her captors with her beauty and charm. Can the young page secure her release where all other plans have failed? An intriguing tale.

The Lothian Run

Mollie Hunter

It is 1736, and Sandy, a young lawyer's apprentice, becomes involved in tracking down a dangerous band of smugglers, who are linked to a Jacobite coup. His several close escapes all add to this compelling adventure story.

Kelpies